the**ashleys**

lip gloss jungle

more books by
melissa de la cruz

The Ashleys series
The Ashleys
Jealous?
Birthday Vicious

Angels on Sunset Boulevard

The Au Pairs series
The Au Pairs
Skinny-Dipping
Sun-Kissed
Crazy Hot

melissa de la cruz

theashleys
lip gloss jungle

aladdin mix

NEW YORK   LONDON   TORONTO   SYDNEY

ALADDIN MIX

Simon & Schuster Children's Publishing Division

1230 Avenue of the Americas, New York, NY 10020

Copyright © 2008 by Melissa de la Cruz

All rights reserved, including the right of reproduction in

whole or in part in any form.

ALADDIN PAPERBACKS, ALADDIN MIX, and related logo are

registered trademarks of Simon & Schuster, Inc.

Designed by Karin Paprocki

The text of this book was set in MrsEavesRoman.

Manufactured in the United States of America

First Aladdin MIX edition November 2008

2 4 6 8 10 9 7 5 3

Library of Congress Control Number 2008921950

ISBN-13: 978-1-4169-3409-7

ISBN-10: 1-4169-3409-X

For Emily Meehan

and Courtney Bongiolatti,

who totally rule!

"Dominance hierarchy: The dominance of one member of a group as measured by superiority in aggressive encounters and order of access to food, mates, resting sites, and other objects that promote survivorship."

—*Animal Behavior Desk Reference*, **Edward M. Barrows**

First class
Up in the sky
Poppin' champagne
Livin' the life . . .
And I won't change
For the glamorous, oh the flossy, flossy.
—Fergie, "Glamorous"

the ashleys
lip gloss
jungle

1

YOU SAY YOU WANT
A REVOLUTION?

IT WAS JUST OVER A MONTH SINCE ASHLEY Spencer's blowout Super-Sweet Thirteen birthday party, and Lauren Page was still recovering from the excess of that celebration, not to mention exhaustion from her "relaxing" winter vacation in the Italian Alps. Her mother had determined that they would become part of the international jet set and had spent all of winter break dragging her family to a host of balls and benefits.

Lauren was glad to be back home for the first day of the spring semester. But she'd overslept that morning and was late meeting the other Ashleys—Miss Spencer herself, plus best friends Ashley "A.A." Alioto and Ashley "Lili" Li—at the Fillmore Starbucks. In fact, she was so late that all the other girls already had their venti decaf soy lattes, each cup nestled into a matching pink cozy (designed by Ashley and handwoven by an artisans' collective in Ecuador), and were waiting impatiently to climb the hill to Miss Gamble's school.

There wasn't even time for Lauren to order a drink—not that she particularly liked decaf soy lattes. But that wasn't the point. Being in the Ashleys meant being the *same* as the Ashleys, right down to holding the cup in your left hand as a way of showcasing the Cartier Love bracelet that Ashley had gifted them with over the holidays.

"I almost took today off," Ashley told them, leading the way up the street, her glossy blond hair bouncing in a high, sleek ponytail. "Cooper and I had the most amazing time yesterday. He knows all the best places in the city. We had the yummiest pizza in North Beach." Cooper was Ashley's new boyfriend. He was supposed to be some Greek shipping heir or something. Ashley kept mentioning he had a yacht.

"North Beach?" Lili wrinkled her pert little nose. "Since when do you hang out in North Beach, Ash?"

"Don't worry, I'm not trying to wrestle away your Miss Boho title," Ashley sniffed. Lauren suppressed a smile. There was nothing remotely bohemian about Lili. Her dark hair was always perfectly coiffed. Her school uniform looked like it was steam-pressed every night, and her patent leather Louboutin Mary Janes shone like a polished mirror.

2

"You guys, it's too early for fighting," protested A.A., who seemed very distracted this morning. Kind of dreamy—though, Lauren thought, A.A. often seemed to have her head in the clouds, just because she was so tall. "But Ash, what were you doing in the city? I thought you guys went to St. Barts like always."

"No, we were here the whole time. My mom didn't feel like traveling." Ashley shrugged. "Anyway, is Max still giving you the silent treatment, Lil?"

Lili nodded sadly.

"I have to *do* something," she said, almost to herself, frowning down at the sidewalk. "I heard from my cousin who transferred to Reed that Max thought I was dating another guy behind his back! Can you imagine?"

Lauren felt sorry for her. Lili really seemed to like this guy Max, even though he went to Arthur Reed Prep School for the Arts, and not Gregory Hall, like all the Ashley SOA (Seal of Approval) boys.

Things were hard enough going out with a Gregory Hall boy, Lauren thought, especially ones like her boyfriend, Christian, who was busy with some sort of team practice at every spare moment. But trying to make it work with someone who went to a weirdo school—someone whose pseudo-alterno friends hated you, someone your parents had forbidden you ever to see again—had to be much more difficult.

"Hello!" Ashley swung around to admonish her entourage. "I haven't finished my story yet! And we're only going to have, like, five minutes on the bench today because Lauren didn't make it on time!"

"Sorry," Lauren called. Sitting on the stone bench outside Miss Gamble's every morning was an important Ashleys tradition. From their throne near the front steps, the Ashleys could sit in fashion judgment on all the other girls trooping into school. It was their major bonding activity, not to mention (according to Ashley) a public service. How else would the students of the city's most exclusive private girls' school know if they were up to snuff?

Ashley picked up her pace, tromping up the hill in her killer heels, and Lauren scurried to keep up, wishing her bag wasn't so heavy. The regulation Ashleys accessory was currently an Uptown or Downtown bag by Yves Saint Laurent. The bags looked great, but neither was really practical for school, since you couldn't sling either one over your shoulder. Oh well, Lauren couldn't jeopardize her hard-won Ashley status by buying the wrong bag. Not right now, anyway, when she still had a secret mission to accomplish: dethrone the Ashleys.

Last year the Ashleys didn't even know her name: Lauren was just one of those invisible dorks who got attention only when she snagged all the academic awards on

Prize Day. But the summer before seventh grade, Lauren's computer-geek dad hit the Internet jackpot, launching the family into the ranks of the mega-rich. The newfound wealth meant that Lauren was able to hit the "makeover" button hard. New hair (literally—her extensions alone cost in the five figures), new skin (spray-tanned weekly), new body (courtesy of a demanding physical trainer—how else do you get rid of baby fat?), new wardrobe (hello, Dior!), and a whole new attitude.

She was determined to use her money for good (like Bono) and change the world. She'd start with the seventh grade (charity begins at home, after all), by infiltrating the Ashleys' ranks. So far, she'd succeeded in becoming one of them by getting them to pretend she was their friend for the sake of starring in a reality television show. The show was canceled halfway through the season, but somehow Lauren remained one of them for real without anyone noticing there was no more need to keep pretending.

Once Lauren got to know the Ashleys, however, she found there were cracks in her "foolproof" plan of social destruction. For one thing, she hadn't counted on *liking* them. The Ashleys might be bratty and superior, but they could also be funny and fun to be around. Ashley's three-ring circus of a birthday party had been a blast, and Lauren realized she would never have met her boyfriend (or had the opportunity to get back together with him) if it weren't for the Ashleys.

"Maybe Lauren was out with Christian last night." Lili darted an insolent look at Ashley's narrow back. "You're not the *only* one who has a boyfriend, you know."

"No, um, I was just home . . . doing stuff," Lauren said quickly, before Ashley and Lili could start bickering again.

"What, like playing dress-up with your new *bestie*?" Ashley clearly intended to punish Lauren for committing the worst possible crime: arriving *after* Ashley at Starbucks. Ashley liked to make a grand entrance with her adoring troops already assembled. Ashley made other people wait, not the other way around.

Lauren's stomach churned nervously. It was the first time Ashley had ever mentioned that she'd noticed Lauren hanging out with Sadie Graham, her former best friend, who had returned to Miss Gamble's earlier last semester.

"By the way, what is up with that girl?" asked A.A., licking soy foam off her lips. "One minute she's a loser nobody, and the next she's posing and pouting like she's Vanessa Hudgens! Before we left for break, I accidentally walked into her in the corridor on Friday, and she was all in my face, telling me to watch out. Actually, what she said was, 'Watch where you're going, Yao Ming!'"

"No!" chorused Lili and Ashley, united in their outrage.

Nothing brought the Ashleys together like an attack from outside their exclusive ranks.

"Where does she get off?" asked Lauren, just as annoyed as they were. Really, she didn't know whether to laugh or cry. The new Sadie Graham was her own creation: Lauren had groomed, manicured, plucked, moisturized, dressed, and designed her—or at least, supervised all of the above by the most expensive stylists in the country doing so.

It had seemed so simple: If Sadie became one of the Ashleys, the two of them could cause in-fighting and suspicion, breaking up the band. Then the girls of Miss Gamble's would be free from the tyranny of the Ashleys forever, making the Ashleys regular girls who didn't feel the need to lord it over everyone else. A clique-free seventh grade! At least, that was the dream.

But this particular dream wasn't really working out just yet. Sure, Sadie had turned into a Scarlett Johansson clone overnight. But the new look seemed to come with a whole new personality.

The Sadie Lauren knew was a smart, normal, down-to-earth girl who just needed to get rid of the glasses and the baggy clothes. Maybe all that French shampoo and flat-ironing had gone to her head, because since Ashley's party, Sadie was revealing herself as a boy-mad megalomaniac. And so much for gratitude—in almost a month she'd barely spoken to

Lauren, when without Lauren's style intervention she'd still be a seventh grader *non grata* at Miss Gamble's.

"How dare she call you a genetic freak?" Ashley was fuming. "Before my party, she looked like an owl who'd been left out in the rain! And she doesn't look much better now, IMHO."

"More like a spaniel," sniffed A.A., swinging her over-stuffed YSL bag as though she wanted to bowl Sadie Graham to the ground with it. "One of those stupid, small King Charles ones with the pudgy faces and flappy ears."

"Or maybe a raccoon," agreed Lili. "Especially with all that mascara she wears. She thinks she's all that, but really, she's just roadkill."

"Yeah," said Lauren. "Like a skunk."

"She is kind of smelly." Ashley giggled. "Cheap perfume! I can smell it from here."

"Right." A.A. laughed, tossing her empty cup into a trash can with ease. The ivy-covered stone facade of Miss Gamble's loomed before them, a soft gray in the hazy winter light.

"No, I really can smell it from here. Excuse me?" Ashley stopped suddenly in her tracks, and they all stumbled into her, like bumper cars reaching a dead end.

"OMG!" gasped Lili.

"You gotta be kidding me." A.A. shook her head so violently that one of her pigtails nearly took out Lauren's eye. Lauren peered over Lili's head to see what the trouble was.

Was some notice posted on the double front doors banning heels higher than three inches or the wearing of James Perse T-shirts under their regulation V-neck school sweaters?

Oh no. Lauren could see: It was something much, much worse.

The Bench of Judgment—the Ashleys' sacred space, reserved for them alone, was currently occupied. Lauren blinked. Were her eyes deceiving her? That girl dressed in a ruffled white blouse over a stylishly A-line plaid uniform skirt, her fingers thrumming a bronze metallic, gold-chained Marc Jacobs bag, her legs outstretched to reveal long gray-and-black argyle socks and a sharp pair of sleek, ankle-length Jimmy Choo booties. Was that really Sadie Graham?

And next to her, the girl with the adorable Katie Holmes bob, her bangs pinned back with a glinting barrette . . . that wasn't Sheridan Riley, was it? As in Ashleys-wannabe, fawning sycophant Sheridan Riley?

Last semester, Sheridan's bangs were still too short, and her handbag was a Fendi Spy, because all she wanted to do was to be an Ashley. Okay, sure, maybe Sheridan had donned a pair of knee-high boots just like the ones Sadie was wearing the last week of class, and Lauren remembered seeing Sheridan saving Sadie a seat in Latin, but she hadn't thought too much of it.

But obviously a decision had been made over break. Sheridan's hair was now a radiant, silvery blond, and the bag sitting next to her on the bench, which she was stroking like it was a pedigreed cat, was the new Louis Vuitton tote, with red patent leather straps and trim. Lauren gulped: Her mother was still on the waiting list for that bag! How?? Why?? And what were these girls doing sitting on the bench?

It was like a standoff in an old Western. Sadie and Sheridan looked over at the Ashleys and exchanged meaningful glances, as if to say, *Game on*. Lili's mouth was an O of surprise, and A.A. was tapping one foot on the ground with irritation, but nobody said anything. Nothing like this had ever happened before in the history of Miss Gamble's, as far as Lauren knew. She couldn't help shivering. Ashley would never stand for this. There might be blood.

"Thanks so much for heating our seats for us, ladies," Ashley said, in her most sarcastic voice. "But pish pish! The main attraction's arrived. Time for the warm-up act to move on."

She gestured with her latte cup toward the stairs. But Sheridan and Sadie didn't move. They just looked at each other again and giggled.

"If you want ringside seats, you'd better arrive earlier," Sadie said, coolly crossing her ankles. "It's standing room only now."

"In fact, you'd look good standing behind us," gushed Sheridan. "No, really! You're so matchy-matchy. You'd make a perfect backup band."

Lauren felt her own mouth drop open. Did Sadie and Sheridan have *any idea* of what they were getting themselves into? Destroying the Ashleys took subtlety and behind-the-scenes manipulation. Not some two-girl revolution before class on a Monday morning.

"I can't believe you, of all people, are daring to criticize *us*," retorted Ashley, though it wasn't clear if she was speaking to Sheridan or Sadie. She dropped her bag on the ground and settled her hands on her slender hips.

"Why?" Sadie stopped smiling. "Because you think you're beyond criticism? Because you think you're the only ones with a sense of style? Because you think you *own* this bench? The only thing you girls own is a set of yesterday's bags and matching pairs of black tights."

"Yeah," snickered Sheridan. She'd obviously grown a new spine, Lauren thought. Could Sadie really have talked her into this? "Mary Janes are *so* sixth grade. And didn't the Olsen twins stop dressing alike when they were six?"

"I think it was about the same time they stopped wearing *pigtails*," said Sadie, staring straight at A.A., who looked too outraged to speak.

"And matching pink nail polish." Sheridan sighed.

"Dude, that Love bracelet? So last season," said Sadie, glancing disdainfully at Lauren. A cluster of girls wandered by, slowing their steps so they could watch the showdown between the Ashleys and their impostors. Usually everyone raced past the bench as fast as they could, to avoid fashion critiques. Today, however, nobody seemed to be in a hurry. Half of Miss Gamble's was hanging out on the steps, listening intently to what was going on.

Lauren knew she should be pleased with this strange turn of events. After all, this was what she'd been working toward all last semester—the downfall of the Ashleys. But right now all she could feel was righteous indignation.

Sadie was nobody until Lauren had started helping her. And Sheridan always seemed perfectly content to play bridesmaid, basking in the glow of the Ashleys' acceptance. Now here they were, mocking the very people whom they themselves had wanted to be—just last semester! It was audacious, all right. And it was just *wrong*. Lauren didn't feel proud of Sadie, or warm toward Sheridan. She just felt incredibly frustrated. She'd wanted to destroy the Ashleys, yes, but not so that another snotty clique could take their place.

The bell for first period started chiming.

"Ta ta!" Sadie waved her fingers at the Ashleys. "Better hurry into class now, like good little matching sheep! Wave good-bye to the Little Match Girls, Sher!"

Lauren bristled. She'd been a friend to Sadie when nobody else would give her old friend the time of day, especially not Sheridan Riley. Her plan was to turn Sadie into an ally, not an enemy, and certainly not into a snob monster who was even worse than . . . well, Ashley Spencer.

Worse than Ashley Spencer? Was there such a thing?

2

ASHLEY DIALS *LOVELINE,*
A.A. HANGS UP

A.A.! WAIT UP!"

A.A. barely heard Ashley. She was still thinking about the strange scene outside on the bench with those upstarts Sheridan Riley and what's-her-name Graham. This was the weirdest thing to happen on a Monday morning since A.A.'s ex-model mother shook her awake early one Monday three years ago and told her that a team from *Harper's Bazaar* was on its way to use her bedroom for a photo shoot. A.A. had to scramble into her school uniform in the bathroom. By the time she peeked her head around the door, her bedroom in the penthouse suite of the Fairmont Hotel was overrun with the photographer's assistants, stylists, hairdressers, models, and a giant Saint Bernard dog.

"We're going to be late," she told Ashley, trying to ignore

the tug at her elbow. Mr. Carroll, the school's only male teacher, got all huffy if anyone was a second late for math. Not that it would make a difference. Ashley didn't care about being late for class. What she cared about, A.A. knew, was being Queen Bee of the school. And this morning a swarm of killer bees was trying to take over the hive.

"I need to talk to you about something important," Ashley whispered fiercely, so A.A. let herself be pulled into one of the paneled oak alcoves of Miss Gamble's main corridor.

"We can talk about it at lunch," said A.A., leaning against the smooth ridges of the polished wall. "If they haven't taken over our table in the refectory, that is."

"Who?" Ashley frowned.

"Sheridan and what's-her-face. You know!"

"Oh, *them.*" Ashley glowered. "Those mall rats better not try a stunt like that again. If they think being alpha girls is as easy as buying a new bag, they're so wrong." She shook her head, her dangling Peruvian earrings brushing her Peter Pan collar. She lowered her voice. "Don't worry, we have plenty of time to deflate *their* balloons. That's not what I want to talk about now. This is about you and me."

A.A. tried to keep calm. *This* was the moment Ashley was choosing to come clean? Two minutes before class was due to start, she wanted to tell all, at long last, about her breakup with Tri Fitzpatrick? A.A. couldn't believe it. She'd been waiting for Ashley to fess up about the whole Tri incident and admit what A.A. already knew—that Tri had dumped Ashley because of his feelings for A.A. and not the other way around, as Ashley had told everybody.

Ashley had pulled off a cover-up more amazing than Jessica Simpson with a bottle of Proactiv, just so she didn't have to turn up solo to the *Preteen Queen* premiere party. If Tri hadn't blabbed all, A.A. would still be in the dark.

Once upon a time, she thought she had feelings for Tri— she'd certainly felt ill every time she'd seen him with Ashley. After they had kissed at a party, A.A. was sure they would get together. Instead, due to Ashley's shenanigans, A.A. thought Tri didn't like her, and Tri had assumed the same, and they ended up dating other people. When Tri had finally told her the truth at Ashley's birthday party, A.A. had been shocked. Too shocked to even figure out what she felt—if anything— about him anymore.

More important, wasn't Ashley supposed to be one of her best friends?

"What is it?" A.A. asked, her voice tense. An apology from Ashley was way overdue.

"It's about . . . a boy," whispered Ashley. A.A. nodded, trying to look like this was No Big Deal. And it wasn't, really— not now, anyway. She and Tri weren't going out, but they weren't enemies. They were buddies who could hang out together, just like they'd been before the ruckus started. A.A. still didn't know if she was relieved or sad.

Ashley was darting looks up and down the emptying corridor.

"Well, what is it?" demanded A.A., unable to hide her impatience a second longer.

"Okay, okay!" Ashley agreed. "This isn't easy for me, you know!"

"I know." A.A. almost felt bad for her. Saying she was wrong was the hardest possible thing for Ashley. But A.A. was glad her friend was finally going to tell her the truth, if only for the sake of keeping their friendship. For a while there, A.A. had seriously considered confronting Ashley with what she knew, but A.A. hated scenes of any kind.

"You know I hate having to ask advice on boys." Ashley flashed a coy smile. "Especially since Cooper's my second boyfriend. So I do have tons of experience."

Oh.

That was what Ashley wanted to talk about?

She should've known. Ashley wasn't going to talk about what had happened with Tri. It was just Cooper, Cooper, Cooper. Ashley could barely talk about anything else.

"Uh-huh." A.A. shifted from one foot to the other, annoyed.

"It's just . . . You know more about kissing than I do.

Don't look at me like that! You do. You're the one who's always making out with guys at parties."

A.A. shook her head, too indignant to speak.

"We haven't really kissed yet." Ashley was still talking, stroking her long golden ponytail absentmindedly. "I mean, don't get me wrong—we've kissed. He kissed me on my birthday. But we haven't *kissed*, if you know what I'm saying."

Ew! The last thing A.A. wanted to listen to right now was Ashley's true romance confessions.

"Cooper keeps telling me he's 'not really in a relationship mode right now.' Do you know what he's talking about?" Ashley asked, leaning closer. "I'm not fluent in Boy."

"I dunno. Maybe it means he's not that into you," A.A. told her. "Maybe he's not sure about you."

Ashley looked horrified. "Of course he's totally into me!" she protested. "It can't possibly be that!"

"Well then." A.A. sighed, already bored with this conversation. What was it her mother was always saying to justify the end of her relationships? "Maybe he's, like, scared of intimacy."

"What's scary about being intimate with me?" Ashley thundered. She clapped one hand over her mouth and shot looks up and down the corridor. Most of the other girls were already safely inside their classrooms.

"Nothing," said A.A., hoping she sounded sincere.

"So what's his deal?" Ashley asked, her high-glossed lower lip rolling into a self-pitying pout.

"Some guys like to take things slow," A.A. offered.

"It's not like I'm *fast* or something!"

"Or maybe he's nervous about getting close to a girl."

"He should be *honored* to get close to me! What else?"

"Well," A.A. said, racking her brain. "Maybe he's just really inexperienced and is worried you might judge him."

"Hello! He knows he's the first boy I've ever kissed!"

"Or maybe he's had a difficult relationship before." *The way you made things difficult for Tri,* A.A. wanted to say. *The way you wouldn't let him break up with you.*

"This is the best relationship he's ever going to have," announced Ashley, shaking her head at Cooper's foolishness. A.A. was getting tired of this. Everything she suggested Ashley shot down.

"Look, do you want my help or not?" A.A. asked.

"Of course! It's just that everything you've come up with so far is totally out of the question. That's why the whole thing is such a mystery to me. There's no logical reason why Cooper is worried about getting into a relationship with me."

"Guys aren't always very logical," A.A. told her. Really, this was true. Who knew what was going on in their stupid heads?

"Ladies!" It was Miss Moos, the dowdy school secretary who looked like she'd bought her hair weave at a Halloween store. A.A. hadn't heard her approaching, maybe because Miss Moos always wore fugly fleece slippers inside the building. That way, A.A. reckoned, she could slither around like a snake and frighten people. "No dawdling in the corridors! You're late for class."

Miss Moos was right: They were more than five minutes late, which meant Mr. Carroll would be practically frothing at the mouth when they arrived. But when A.A. and Ashley pushed open the heavy classroom door and hurried toward their usual leather-padded seats at the back of the classroom, A.A. barely noticed crotchety Mr. Carroll. She dimly heard his grumpy admonishments for them to take their seats at once and turn to a page in the textbook. She was too busy staring at a piece of paper she found on her desk.

"Did you see this?" hissed Ashley next to her. She had received one too.

A.A. nodded.

It was a list, typed on a computer, with the mystifying heading "The S. List." She could see at a glance that it was a list of what was in and out at Miss Gamble's.

In the "In" column were the usual suspects: Ksubi jeans, iPhones, the junior varsity water polo team at Gregory Hall. The "Out" list wasn't much of a surprise either: It included Hannah Montana, the Spelt Bread Diet, and vacations anywhere in the lower forty-eight states.

But it was the items at the bottom of the page that had made A.A. stop in her tracks. The last line read, "In: The S.

Society," and on the other side was the final shocking item, "Out: The Ashleys (and Lauren)."

Her phone buzzed, and she checked it underneath the desk. It was a text from Ashley: THE ASHLEYS OUT? SINCE WHEN?

A.A. sighed. She had a good idea who was behind the so-called S. Society. And while she usually didn't care too much about the Ashleys' vaunted social standing, she was miffed to find they were being openly dissed by their peers.

Were the Ashley as last season as blobby, shapeless baby-doll dresses? Was their glorious reign at Miss Gamble's truly over?

3

MAX GOES BACK TO BLACK

ALL THE ASHLEYS—INCLUDING LAUREN—
were in an uproar. They'd talked about
nothing but this mysterious S. List all
through lunch, surreptitiously texting one another in
afternoon classes with indignant questions about the so-
called S. Society. And Lili had joined in—of course she
had. She was an Ashley, first and foremost.

Although lately, Lili really couldn't care less about the
Ashleys' golden reputation. Sure, the usurping of the bench
that morning by pretenders Sheridan Riley and Sadie
Graham was obnoxious. And the "anonymous" in/out list was
irritating. But she had *way* more important things on her
mind right now—like really missing Max.

Usually Lili enjoyed school: She aced all her classes and
was reigning queen of the Honor Board. Today, however,
dragged by. The second the final bell rang, she bid a quick

good-bye to her friends, grabbed her YSL bag, slipped her brand-new BlackBerry Pearl into her blazer pocket, and rushed out the front door of Miss Gamble's.

Her heart was jittering the way it always was when she left school for the day. Because even though she knew things were all over with Max—her first real boyfriend—Lili still hoped, deep down, that when she emerged onto the elegant stone steps of Miss Gamble's, he'd be waiting outside.

The kids from Reed Prep got out way early, and a long time ago, when they were still dating, Max used to meet Lili after school whenever it was possible. That is, whenever her mother—the ferocious Nancy Khan (who insisted on a boyfriend ban after finding out about Lili's co-ed camping trip) wasn't picking her up from school for one of Lili's dozen after-school enrichment activities. Back then, Max would be hanging out across the street, flipping his skateboard with one foot, looking adorably scruffy and handsome.

The kids at Reed Prep didn't have to wear uniforms, so Max was usually wearing a cool pair of faded jeans and a khaki army jacket, the red emblem on his Chrome messenger bag glinting in the sun. According to Ashley, he looked homeless—which he totally wasn't—and according to A.A., he looked like kind of a doofus, showing off with his skateboard, which he *so* wasn't. What did they know?

Of course they preferred preppie Gregory Hall boys, who were obsessed with sports. In Pacific Heights, everyone had to fit into the same little box: They all dressed the same, they looked the same, their families belonged to all the same country clubs. Just like those social climbers had said that morning: The Ashleys always had to match. Well, maybe Lili was tired of being the same as everyone else.

She stood on the front steps, peering across the street, hoping against hope, even though it had been months since Max had waited for her, while girls pushed past her, everyone hurrying down to the parade of BMWs and Porsche SUVs waiting to pick them up. No Max—of course. He hadn't been there since forever. She'd been furious when her cousin (a huge gossip) told her those skanky friends of his had told him a whole lot of bad things about her, including that she was seeing some Gregory Hall guy on the side. It had practically ruined her winter break—she'd felt none of the joy she usually did when she saw the piles of presents under the tree at Christmas.

How could he think that she was cheating on him? That totally explained why he'd been so aloof at Ashley's party. He hadn't even believed her when she said she'd been grounded all week.

She lingered on the steps, forlorn and almost tearful. Usually on a Monday, Lili was driven to the Alliance

Française for an hour of Advanced French Conversation, where she could be sure of seeing Max—he was the only other pupil in Madame LeBrun's tutorial. But Madame LeBrun had canceled all sessions for two weeks while she returned to France for her niece's wedding. Suddenly there was a gaping hole in Lili's Monday afternoon schedule—no French and, much worse, no Max.

Her mother had to take Lili's small twin sisters, Josephine and Brennan, to the pediatric psychologist this afternoon for preschool IQ testing, so Lili had a rare window of freedom. Nancy was going to collect her outside the Fillmore Starbucks in half an hour. Lili had considered asking one of the Ashleys to hang out there with her, but for now all she wanted was to be alone. All this chatter about the S. Society was just so much hot air. Her personal life was falling apart, and nobody seemed to care!

Lili marched off down the tree-lined hill, past the elegant row of renovated Victorian mansions. Maybe she would go to Starbucks and do some online research for her biology project. Or maybe she'd read another chapter of their honors English novel. Or maybe she'd just enjoy a café mocha, something she couldn't do with the Ashleys, since they all had to get Ashley's favorite drink: the soy latte, which tasted like extra hot crap, in her humble opinion.

She pondered her options and decided that what she

really wanted to do was take a casual stroll . . . one that might take her past the dive-y diner off Fillmore where Max and his friends liked to hang out. Really, she could use some fresh air after too many stuffy hours locked inside Miss Gamble's.

Lili scooted past the door of Starbucks and kept walking, trying to tell herself she was just going for an innocent walk, rather than desperately trying to track Max down, like some psycho stalker. There wasn't any harm in walking for a few more blocks, was there?

Although the diner was less than ten minutes' walk from Starbucks, Lili felt like it was a different world. She remembered the last time she was there—more than two months ago, which felt like an eternity. All she'd wanted to do then was hang out with Max and (if she was honest with herself) impress him. Lili sighed, scuffing her Mary Janes along the sidewalk. Well, *that* certainly hadn't worked out.

She'd agreed to go on a camping trip that had turned into a nightmare, from the near attack by a bear—which no one else saw—to the flooding of the campsite, to the super-grounding she got when her parents found out about the trip. Not to mention having to spend time with his loser goth friends and their bitchy girlfriends, Cassandra and Jezebel.

Speaking of whom . . . rounding the corner, Lili caught a horrifying glimpse of what looked suspiciously like the dyed-red hair of Cassandra Allison. She was sashaying into the diner, laughing her horrible horsey laugh. Lili shuddered and instinctively ducked into another store doorway. Weedy, whiny Cassandra was one person Lili *never* wanted to see again.

Why did Max have such atrocious friends? He didn't seem to have anything in common with them. Max was friendly and sweet and smart, while his friends were a bunch of irritating posers. Was it just because they all liked the same kind of music? What kind of friendship was that? Then she wondered if she was friends with the Ashleys because they all liked the same kind of clothes.

Lili edged along the street, pretending to look in store windows. Not that she wanted to buy *anything* for sale on this block, which mainly seemed to consist of tattoo parlors, incense-scented boutiques that featured marijuana-leaf-design T-shirts, and costume shops that sold cheap, brightly colored wigs that probably made your head itch after five minutes.

With every step, she drew nearer to the diner, with its dirty windows and cracked awning, and her heart started thudding and skipping like a maniac. She tried to act oh-so-casual as she crept up to the window—obscured, she hoped, by the chipped letters spelling out the diner's name across the glass (appropriately enough, it was called Garage)—and paused to peek through the gap between the final G and the E.

Max was there.

He was sitting in one of the diner's vinyl booths with his buddies Jason and Quentin. Though he had his back to Lili, she could tell it was him—she'd know those cowlicks in his platinum blond hair anywhere. Just seeing the back of his head made her feel stupidly weak in the knees.

Cassandra was standing at the end of the table, telling some (no doubt) boring story and running a hand through her stringy hair. Her BFF Jezebel was snuggled up to Jason, picking at her pierced nostril. Quentin, Cassandra's boyfriend, sat on the other side of Jezebel, gazing up at Cassualty with his usual dense, slack-jawed expression. Lili pressed her button nose against the glass. But who was sitting next to Max, wriggling out of her seat to join Cassandra? It was hard to see, but it kind of looked like . . . it looked like . . .

A girl.

Someone with long, super-straight hair dyed inky black. Someone tall and thin, wearing striped leggings and a tatty sweater dress, a studded black belt slung around her non-existent waist, climbing out of the booth and standing hip to hip with Cassandra. Someone blowing a kiss at Max and tinkling her fingers at him. Lili's heart dropped to her stomach.

Max turned to look at Amy Winehouse Lite. Lili knew that look too well. It was the look Max used to give her when they were together. What was he doing? Blowing a kiss back at Amy? No!

Lili was outraged. They'd only broken up *yesterday* (okay, a month ago, but still!) and Max had already found himself a new girlfriend. Not only that, he'd chosen the complete anti-Lili. She had thought the whole drama between them was just a horrible misunderstanding, something that could be fixed with a good heart-to-heart, once she was able to tell him her side of the story when she got back from Aspen. But now she realized the truth. Max *wanted* the breakup, because he already had Miss Rocker Chick waiting in the wings.

A tear dripped down her cheek. She'd been wasting her time, wishing for a reconciliation with Max. He was with his own kind now, having a great time. He didn't need Lili. He obviously didn't miss her. It was all over.

Then the worst possible thing happened. Cassandra suddenly looked toward the window and . . . omigod! She must have spotted Lili, because her face lit up in a malicious, delighted smile. Lili could see Cassandra mouthing her name, tugging on Groupie Girl's arm and pointing.

Lili took off down the street as fast as she dared in her perilous heels. Why had she hung around so long? She'd totally humiliated herself in front of the odious Reed Prep loserati. And she was probably late getting to Starbucks. Her mother would be furious, especially considering that Lili had been on virtual house arrest since the disastrous camping trip from hell.

"Lili!"

She glanced back over her shoulder. Max was standing outside the diner, one hand up in the air, as though he was stopping traffic. There was no way she was going back there for more humiliation. Everything was over with Max, so talking to him would be totally pointless.

"Lili!"

She turned away from him without answering, wobbling away as fast as she could. There was nothing to talk about. The picture at the diner was crystal clear. All she had to do was keep putting one foot in front of the other. All she had to do was keep running away.

4

MOVING CRIBS IS NEVER EASY

'M HOME!" ASHLEY CALLED, BUT THE ONLY REPLY
she got was from the butler who'd opened the door for
her. Her footsteps echoed though the grand marble
entryway as she marched toward the great room, the scene
of her brilliant descent-by-trapeze a month ago. Ashley
sighed with contentment at the memory of her total triumph. The entire seventh grade at Miss Gamble's had
been blown away by her Super-Sweet Thirteen birthday
extravaganza.

But now all everyone was obsessed with was this stupid
S. Society and that even more yawnworthy S. List. Ashley
knew what S really stood for—a load of crap!

But you couldn't really blame everyone for talking: *She*
couldn't think about much else either. The nerve of that
Sadie Nobody, turning up to school in argyle socks and
booties! Ashley been planning the exact same thing for the

Ashleys, and now she'd have to come up with something new. There was no way they could be fashion followers.

Ashley felt her face crumple into a frown, her mood suddenly as gray as the clouds rolling over San Francisco Bay— the view from the great room's twelve-foot windows. Why were other people so intent on spoiling Ashley's perfect life? They were all so mean and jealous. Well, at least she was home now, among her peeps. That is, her devoted parents, their huge staff, and her gorgeous labradoodle puppy, Princess Dahlia von Fluffsterhaus.

"Mommy!" Ashley shrieked, her voice echoing around the cavernous room. "Where are you?"

"She's upstairs, Miss Ashley." The butler loomed in the doorway, the last of the afternoon sun glinting in his silver hair. "In *your* room, I believe."

In *her* room? Ashley picked up her Uptown bag and made for the broad staircase. She hoped her mother wasn't going through one of her let's-give-away-all-our-clothes-to-charity phases. The last time that happened, Ashley came home from school to find her room a maze of black trash bags, all filled with clothes her mother thought she didn't need anymore.

Hello! Having clothes wasn't about need, it was about must—as in, must-have. It was about freedom of choice. Freedom! That's right, Ashley thought, growing more indignant with every step: Having a huge walk-in closet and dressing room (stocked with every fashionable brand on the planet, 150 pairs of shoes, a bag for every week of the year, and a forest of accessory trees) was her personal right as an American.

She didn't mind giving one of the maids a hand-me-down from time to time, but she totally objected to raids on her personal collection every time her mother got a pang of liberal guilt. Didn't Matilda Spencer realize that Ashley was under assault every day of her life by Ashley haters, the kind of people who were dying to see her in the same outfit twice, or—even worse—inadequately accessorized?

Ashley took the last two steps in one giant stride. Another raid on her personal space was quite possible: Ever since her parents told her that her mother was pregnant—ugh!—with another, unwanted-by-Ashley mini-Spencer, Matilda had exhibited all kinds of weird behavior.

In the last week alone, Ashley had seen her do the following: (1) weep uncontrollably at a TV commercial featuring puppies playing in a flowery meadow; (2) eat full-fat, nonorganic vanilla ice cream straight from the tub; and (3) sit in the kitchen making a "Baby's First Trimester" scrapbook with the help of Maria, one of the maids, while Maria's wizened grandmother—flown in from San Salvador in a private plane, courtesy of Ashley's father—sat in a rocking chair crocheting baby booties from skeins of nonrecycled angora.

Everyone in this house had gone crazy! Matilda was probably upstairs right now, selecting all of Ashley's cutest outfits to be freighted to the needy throughout Central America. Well, Ashley had needs as well—something everyone in this house seemed to have forgotten.

"Don't even think of . . . ," she began, charging through the double doors that led to her second-floor suite and almost tripping over the furry, reclining form of Princess Dahlia. But the scene that greeted her wasn't what she expected at all. Her closet doors was safely closed, and there weren't any black bags sprouting like rotting fungi all over the handwoven Turkish carpet.

Instead there were two maids, their arms full of her bed linen, and Enrico, the asthmatic handyman, who appeared to be dismantling her antique four-poster bed. Her mother, in a billowy peasant shirt and holey maternity jeans (since they were from when she was pregnant with Ashley), was holding a roll of paper against the wall, beaming at its butterfly pattern. Redecorating without discussion or permission! This was even worse.

"Darling!" Matilda called, her beautiful blue eyes sparkling, her long blond hair loose around her shoulders. "Come and look at this wallpaper! These are handcrafted imitation butterfly wings, woven from silk and dipped in gilt. Aren't they just precious?"

"Mommy," whined Ashley, dumping her bag on the floor inches from her puppy's curly head. "I don't want new wallpaper. And I especially don't want butterflies! It's *très juvenile*. If we're going to redo the walls, I'd rather have those cool chinoiserie silk panels from Shanghai Tang. Remember?"

"Oh, sweetie!" Matilda rolled up the paper and stepped toward her, skirting Enrico's unfolded tool kit. "You can have whatever you want. You know that!"

"Good," said Ashley, smiling smugly. At last someone was listening to her. "Then maybe we could get matching panels for the bed, and one of those lacquered armoires with gold handles."

One of the maids scuttled past, carrying Ashley's favorite silk comforter out the door.

"Well, I'm not sure about that," Matilda said, biting her lip. "The thing is, you may not have the space for this bed *and* a big armoire. In fact, Enrico thinks you won't even have room for the bed."

Enrico scowled at the mention of his name and viciously stabbed at one of the bedpost joints with his screwdriver.

"Why not?" Ashley surveyed the room. They might have to move the flat-screen TV, or get rid of the antique dresser and relocate the chaise, but there was plenty of space in here, really. If her mother would let her rip out the window seats, as she'd been begging for *months*. . . .

"Sweetie, we're moving you upstairs," Matilda explained, one soft hand alighting on Ashley's arm. "Didn't we discuss this already?"

"No, we did not!" Ashley cried. Leave her room? Move upstairs? Hello? Dahlia von Fluffsterhaus woke up with a start and staggered over, rubbing against Ashley's ankles.

"Silly me!" Her mother sighed. "I'm forgetting everything these days. This is just how I was when I was pregnant with you."

Ashley ignored her mother's sappy smile. Tears pricked the corners of her eyes.

"Why don't you just send me away to live with Aunt Agnes?" she asked, meaning the Spencers' only living relative, a batty maiden aunt who lived on a sheep farm in Vermont. Ashley picked up Princess Dahlia and clasped the puppy tightly to her chest. Dahlia squirmed and yapped in protest, wriggling her way back to the floor. Great! Even Ashley's own dog didn't want her.

"Now don't overreact." Matilda dropped the roll of wallpaper onto the chaise, and the other maid took the opportunity to scurry out of the room, trailing a bundle of Ashley's four-hundred-thread-count Egyptian cotton sheets. "When you think about it, you'll realize why we're doing this. Your room is nearer to ours, so it makes sense that the new baby sleep here."

36

"Why can't you turn the music room or the second study into the baby's room? They're right by your room as well."

"But they don't have this lovely light, or an en suite bathroom," Matilda explained. "This is much nicer than any of the other rooms on this floor."

"I know!" Ashley pouted, kicking off her school shoes and secretly hoping that grumpy old Enrico tripped over them. "So why do *I* have to move?"

"Darling," Matilda pleaded. "You know I'm going to have to get up in the middle of the night to nurse every couple of hours. You don't want me walking up and down the stairs all the time, do you?"

Ashley rolled her eyes.

"But you're hiring a baby nurse to do all that middle-of-the-night stuff!" She wanted to see Matilda try to get out of this one. But her mother didn't seem fazed at all.

"That's right." She nodded. "A nurse will be here to *help* me. And that's another reason why we need this room. Your dressing room will be her sitting room, where she can rest and read while the baby is sleeping. It all makes sense."

"Not to me it doesn't!" Ashley fumed. She wanted to throw herself on the floor and cry with rage. This sibling-in-the-making was already ruining her life!

"And you know how pretty and cozy the little guest room is. The chinoiserie silk panels you mentioned will look just darling in there. I'll send for them tomorrow, and . . ."

Matilda was still talking, but Ashley couldn't hear another word. She was being moved upstairs to the little guest room? Not even the main guest room, which was reserved for the VIPs? The little guest room was little with a capital L! It was practically the attic.

". . . it's not *that* much smaller than this room, you know," Matilda was saying. "Sure, it doesn't have a closet, and you have to walk across the hallway to the bathroom. And the ceilings are a little lower, and there's not room for a window seat—"

"Mom," Ashley interrupted her. "You would make a terrible salesperson, okay? You're making it worse, and it's already bad enough."

"Now, now," Matilda chided, smiling. "Just remember, people in Japan live in houses that are much smaller."

"Great!" shrieked Ashley. "Why don't you just give me a roll-up futon and a block of wood for a pillow and stick me in a cupboard!"

Her mother was totally missing the point. It wasn't that the guest room was really tiny, or that it was on another floor. It was that Ashley's domain was *here*, where it had always been, every day of her life. And now she was being ousted by this new baby. It was like the new baby got the top of the podium and she, Ashley, was being shoved into the silver-medal position. If there was one thing Ashley hated, it was being number two.

First the S. Society, now this. A month ago Ashley was on top of the world, soaring on a trapeze and zooming off on a Vespa with Cooper. Now she was ousted from the bench outside Miss Gamble's and evicted from her bedroom. She was a dispossessed person. How could she maintain her top-dog status when she was basically homeless and under attack from all sides?

Ashley felt a tear roll down her cheek. This wasn't life as she knew it, not anymore. Did she still have what it took to be Ashley Spencer?

5

YOUR MISSION, SHOULD YOU
CHOOSE TO ACCEPT IT

T WAS THAT TIME OF YEAR AGAIN. USUALLY LAUREN didn't look forward to it at all, but this year was different. She was one of the Ashleys now, and no matter how many secret societies were forming around them, trying to knock them off their perch, right now was the best time of year to be an Ashley. It was Congé time.

Sure, she could join the S. Society—they seemed just as intent on bringing down the Ashleys as she was, except they weren't doing it for the right reasons. Sadie and Sheridan just wanted to replace the Ashleys, whereas Lauren wanted something more life changing. She wanted not only the Ashleys, but the very *idea* of the Ashleys—that some girls were more equal than others—totally destroyed.

Besides, better to stick with the devil you know than

the devil you don't, Lauren thought. The members of the S. Society were upstarts, and Lauren wanted to enjoy herself just a little bit longer as part of the ruling class. Just for once, couldn't she participate in the annual Mother-Daughter Fashion Show, where the Ashleys were always the star models on the runway? Instead of sitting in the back, picking at her salad and wishing it was over?

And just for once, couldn't she be on the Congé Committee?

Congé was a French tradition adopted by Miss Gamble's, a "free day" in the middle of the spring semester that was a secret surprise for the whole school. Ever since the fifth grade, the Ashleys had ruled the Congé Committee: They got to decide where to take the whole school for the day. Sure, there were older girls on the committee, too—but the Ashleys were so bossy they always ended up getting their way.

Lauren wasn't sure if she'd go that far . . . but the idea of sitting on the committee? Terribly exciting. Every year the Ashleys didn't just know where the school was spending Congé—they were the only ones aware of *when* it was taking place. All the teachers at Miss Gamble's tried to throw students off the scent by assigning a ton of homework and threatening all kinds of arduous tests on that day. But the Ashleys always secretly blew off all the extra work, because they knew it was all a sham. For the first time, Lauren would be in the know as well. For that reason alone, she wanted to stick with the Ashleys at least until the end of the semester.

After classes ended on Wednesday, the Ashleys assembled in the oak-paneled school library. The last time Lauren had been in this room for a meeting, she was defending Ashley against the Honor Board. She'd triumphed then—getting Ashley out of a suspension and persuading her obstinate "client" to invite the entire seventh grade to her birthday party.

Now Lauren slid into one of the black-leather chairs surrounding the vast wooden table and gazed up at the ornate chandelier, trying to suppress a smile. Who knew? Maybe she could triumph again. All she needed to do was come up with a brilliant idea for Congé, and she'd practically rule the school. Maybe then she could call the shots, even among the Ashleys. It was going to be *so nice*, being on the inside of things for once.

"Where is Miss Charm?" complained Ashley, who had been snappy all week. The only thing that seemed to cheer her up was the rain that morning, because it meant that *nobody* could sit on the bench by the school's front steps— even though she insisted that she intended to drag Sadie and Sheridan off it by force if they ever dared sit there again. "Doesn't she know our time is valuable?"

"I'm starving," A.A. moaned, pushing her chair back so

she could stretch her long legs. "Does anyone have any ideas, by the way? Lili?"

"What?" Lili glanced up from her BlackBerry. She'd been frowning at it since they arrived.

"You know, ideas? For Congé?" Ashley gave her ponytail an impatient toss. "Or do I have to do everything, as usual?"

"Hello, girls!" Miss Charm, the etiquette teacher and seventh-grade class adviser, swept into the room, the heavy door clanging shut behind her. She paused for a second to glance at her reflection in the bookshelves' glass doors, lovingly patting her graying beehive. Ashley rolled her eyes, and Lauren tried not to giggle. "Glad to see you all here promptly. We have important things to discuss!" she said brightly.

Lauren sat up straighter, feeling excitement building in her chest, while A.A. only yawned. The other two Ashleys looked just as bored. Lili was putting away her BlackBerry, a wistful expression on her pretty face, and Ashley was scowling at Miss Charm, as if she were planning to have her removed from the school and exiled to some retirement home in another state.

"An exciting time." Miss Charm nodded, lowering herself into the chair at the head of the table and setting a powder pink spiral notebook on the table in front of her. Ashley was right, Lauren thought: Those mock Chanel suits favored by Miss Charm really had to go. "And this year is a time of change."

"Change?" Lili looked up. "What do you mean, 'change'?"

"Yeah, are the eighth-graders actually interested in planning this with us this year?" A.A. asked.

"Oh no, you know our 'seniors' are too busy with prep school applications to bother with this trivia." Miss Charm assured. "But, my dears, I'm afraid all good things must come to an end."

"Not Congé!" gasped A.A., who earlier that day had confided in Lauren that Congé was her favorite thing about Miss Gamble's, especially since the refectory had stopped serving gourmet Italian macaroni and cheese.

"Oh no," Miss Charm reassured her, tapping her clipped nails on the table. "Don't worry about that. But our little committee. Er, there's been some suggestion that we're not quite inclusive enough."

"We're totally inclusive!" Ashley cried. She pointed across the table at Lauren. "We have a new member this year! Whom we invited! Even though she's not, you know, an Ashley!"

Lauren forced a smile. She hoped that Ashley was referring to her first name, not her status within the group.

"Be that as it may," Miss Charm said, holding up one wizened hand, "some *other* students have petitioned the headmistress. They feel, and I'm not saying they're right or wrong, but they feel the Congé Committee has been—how shall I put it?—an exclusive domain for too long."

"Of course it's exclusive!" Ashley made a face. "Duh!"

"If we let in too many people, it'll be harder to keep the whole thing a secret," Lauren pointed out. Taking a practical approach, she decided, might be more effective with teachers—even someone as flighty and irrational as Miss Charm.

"We're at maximum capacity as it is," added Lili briskly.

"I know, I know." Miss Charm closed her eyes and clasped her hands together, as though she was about to lead them in prayer. "But the administration of our wonderful school believes that it's only fair if other people have a voice in the planning of the event."

"So that's why I've come up with a viable solution. Rather than make the Congé Committee too large and unwieldy with additional members, I have suggested a compromise. This year there will be two Congé committees."

"What?" Ashley was indignant. "*Two* committees?"

"And whichever committee comes up with the best plan for the day will be awarded the job of organizing it. We will reveal to both committees the week in which Congé is scheduled, but not the specific date. When your plan—or the other plan—is accepted, then I will reveal that date to the winning committee and all final plans will be made. Is everything clear?"

"Clear as mud," grumbled A.A., tearing out one of her hair bands. "How can we make plans if we don't know the specific date?"

"And how can you trust this other so-called committee not to blab it around the whole school?" Lauren added. She was starting to get a sinking feeling about who this rival committee might be.

"Please, girls," Miss Charm pleaded, looking very flustered. "I can reveal to you now, in total confidence, that Congé is scheduled between March 10 and 15. To fully prepare, your committee leader must present your plans by next month."

"That's me," said Ashley, looking at Lili, who only shrugged.

"I then will discuss it with my fellow teachers, and we will let the successful committee—and the successful committee alone—know forty-eight hours before Congé takes place."

"Sounds good," Lili said confidently. Lauren had heard that it was usually Lili who came up with the Ashleys' Congé plans: She was more organized than Ashley and more focused than A.A. Last year, it had been her idea to book a private steam train through Napa Valley."

"But why do we have to have competition?" Ashley complained.

"Think of it as a new challenge for you!" declared Miss

Charm with a nervous smile. "I'm sure you girls are up to it. I have full confidence in you."

"Hello!" said Ashley, pushing her chair back from the table in aggravation. "Of course you have confidence in us! We're the Congé professionals. Who is this other amateur committee, anyway?"

Miss Charm cleared her throat and flipped open the spiral notebook sitting on the table.

"I believe they are known as . . . ah yes, here it is. The S. Society."

Ashley groaned. "*Just* as I suspected. Well, at least one thing's for sure—we'll definitely win this competition. If we're talking about those idiots, they haven't got an original idea in their heads."

"Now, now, dear," said Miss Charm absentmindedly, gathering up her notebook and heaving herself out of the solid chair. "There's no need for such language. But remember—not a word to anyone!"

As soon as the teacher had left the room, Ashley didn't seem quite so gung ho. "Those little . . . ," she ranted. "It's not a society—it's just Sheridan and that copycat Sally!"

"Sadie," A.A. corrected. Lauren said nothing, shrinking into her seat. The last thing she wanted right now was anyone drawing the connection between her and her awful creation, Sadie Graham.

"Whatever! How dare they try to muscle in on Congé?"

"So we have competition—we'll blow them out of the water," Lili reassured Ashley. But Lauren observed Lili looking a little worried.

"I just thought of something terrible," A.A. moaned, her head lolling back in despair. "If we *don't* win, we'll be just like all the other girls in this school."

"Fashion-backward and lame?" Ashley asked.

"No, I mean out of the loop! We'll have to study for the tests and do all the extra homework that week, because we won't know *when* exactly Congé is going to happen."

"I can't do any more than I'm already doing," Lili whined, pulling out her BlackBerry.

"Could everyone please *focus*?" thundered Ashley. "This is a crisis, in case you've forgotten!" She turned to Lauren. "This is all your fault, by the way!"

"Mine?" Lauren protested. How did Ashley know? Of course it was all her fault. She'd created this mess by convincing Sadie Graham that she could be as chic and confident as any of the Ashleys, not realizing that Sadie would instantly turn against her. But how could Ashley know her secret plan?

"You were the one who talked me into inviting these nobodies to my birthday party. No wonder they're all having delusions of grandeur!" Ashley accused.

Lauren tried not to look too relieved. Ashley was just being overdramatic as usual. She didn't *know*. But she was pretty close to the truth. Lauren had to act quickly to throw off any suspicion. "I have an idea," she declared.

"It better be a good one," Ashley snapped.

"What I . . . what I was thinking was," Lauren said, trying to sound more assured than she felt, "I could try to infiltrate the S. Society. You know, Sadie and I used to be friendly. I could try to find out what they're planning. I'll be an under-cover agent."

"Like Jennifer Garner on *Alias*." Lili seemed to like the idea.

"Wasn't *Alias* canceled?" asked A.A.

"Exactly what we'll do to Lauren if she fails in this mission," said Ashley, gifting Lauren with a particularly threatening smile. "Here's the plan. Lauren, find out what the stupid S. Club is up to. If you don't, you might as well find other people to sit with at the ref."

"She doesn't mean it," A.A. said. Lauren tried to laugh.

"Shut up! The rest of you, start coming up with brilliant ideas for Congé. Our quality of life at Miss Gamble's totally depends on it! If we don't win Congé, we may as well drop out of school."

After this sobering warning, they all filed out of the library in silence, Lauren bringing up the rear.

Unlike A.A., Lauren knew full well that Ashley wasn't joking. She wasn't sure how she was going to do it, but she just had to infiltrate the S. Society and find out what they had planned. Otherwise *she* would be out—out of the Ashleys entirely. So much for all her grand plans this semester.

6

IT'S ALL FUN AND GAMES UNTIL
SOMEONE LOSES HER HEART

A.A. WISHED SHE COULD BE ALL HARD-working like Lili, but when school was over, the last thing she felt like doing was more work. She needed to unwind, especially with all this fuss about Congé and the annoying S. Society.

And she needed to hang out with Tri.

Now that they were friends again, A.A. and Tri had made a pact the week after Ashley's party: They were going to give video games a rest for a while and catch up on the fun stuff they used to do.

"Fun stuff," A.A. knew, was code for "kid stuff," and that was fine with her. Some days she was in no hurry to grow up. In fact, she kind of missed the days when she could just play games and ride bikes with Tri and not . . . well, not *feel* anything.

Feeling things made everything in life more complicated, she decided. Having a boyfriend just wasn't her thing right now, obviously. Let Ashley gush about Cooper, and Lili moan about Max, and Lauren go all dreamy eyed every time Christian's name came up. Who cared? She and Tri were friends, nothing more, nothing less—and that was exactly the way she wanted it.

They met up outside the Fairmont Hotel, where they both lived, A.A. pushing her Raleigh bike, zipping up her nylon jacket to keep the wind out. Tri was messing around in the valet parking area, doing wheelies on his neon green BMX like a pro. A.A. climbed onto her bike and fastened the silver helmet her half brother Ned had given her for her birthday.

"About time!" he shouted, ramming on his own helmet. "It's freezing out. Let's get going." His smile lit up his whole face, and his cheeks were red from the cold.

A.A. thought he looked cuter than ever, with his dark hair falling into his eyes, even though she told herself she wasn't noticing those kinds of things anymore. "Race you down Nob Hill!" she called, whizzing out into the street ahead of him.

They raced down the hill toward Chinatown, dodging cable cars and pedestrians, turning back for a marathon uphill battle. Sometimes A.A. was way ahead; sometimes Tri was.

Even though it was a cold day, it was sunny and bright. Before too long, A.A. was feeling hot and tired—but in a good way, the way she felt after a strenuous game of soccer, when she'd scored a couple of goals. Lauren was always talking about the amazing home gym her family had built, but *this* was A.A.'s idea of exercise—getting out in the fresh air and racing about until she was exhausted. This afternoon she felt happy for the first time in ages. Hanging out with Tri was great. Friendship was much less stressful than having a silly boyfriend.

"Need an afternoon nap?" Tri mocked her, waiting for her at the corner of Jackson and Presidio. His bright blue eyes were twinkling. "Ready to admit defeat?"

"As if!" A.A. gasped. She set both feet on the ground, trying to get her breath back. She needed to play for time. "My helmet's come loose. I have to fix it."

"That old line." Tri rolled his eyes, although he looked pretty worn out himself. A.A. pulled off her helmet and adjusted her two pigtails, bundling them together so they didn't fly into her face when she was riding.

"A.A.! Tri!" Ashley appeared at the door of a boutique, waving frantically at them. "What are you guys doing here?"

"What does it look like?" asked Tri. The smile disappeared from his face.

Ashley ignored him. "A.A., what are you doing to your hair?"

"It keeps blowing into my mouth," A.A. explained. Ashley raised a critical eyebrow. Ashley was wearing a chic little cardigan over pedal pushers, and her hair was newly blown out and shiny. A.A. felt like a slob by comparison.

"You look kind of bizarre, you know. Someone might see you!"

"So?" A.A. felt defensive.

"Someone from the S. Society, for example!" Ashley tapped one foot on the sidewalk. "Do you want them saying the Ashleys run around after school looking like hippies—or boys?"

Tri gave an impatient snort.

"What did you buy?" A.A. asked her quickly.

"*I* didn't buy anything," Ashley complained. She brandished a large white shopping bag, which was tied with pale green ribbon. "My mother is in that store," she said, gesturing with her shoulder, "buying stuff for you-know-who."

"Who?"

"The *baby*," Ashley whispered. She seemed embarrassed every time the subject came up. "I don't know why the stupid thing can't use all my old stuff. It's not even born yet, and it has more clothes and toys than I ever did!"

"I guess."

"And my mother *knows* I need something new to wear for

my date with Cooper on Saturday night. She *knows* how important this relationship is to me."

"Oh." A.A. didn't really know what to say. She felt intensely awkward. Being friends with Ashley was one thing; being friends with Tri was something totally separate and different. Standing together like this on a street corner talking about *relationships* only reminded her that there was something unresolved among the three of them. Something to do with secrets, kisses, and lies. In other words, something A.A. really would rather not think about this afternoon.

Because all she wanted to do today was ride her bike and have some fun, not obsess about grown-up things like kissing and breaking up. But here was Ashley and the real world—or the Ashley version of the real world, anyway—to spoil their fun.

"Hey, I'm just going to get some water." Tri climbed off his bike. "Watch my stuff, okay?"

A.A. nodded, glad that Tri was going to be out of earshot for a few minutes. This whole situation was just too awkward.

"Your mother might be looking for you," she suggested to Ashley.

"She doesn't even know I exist anymore," Ashley sniffed. "Why—are you trying to get rid of me?"

"No—I mean, well . . . it's kind of weird, isn't it? Hanging out with me and Tri? Don't you think? Seeing as you guys broke up and everything."

"Not really." Ashley dismissed that idea with a wave of her hand. "The only weird thing is the way you can hang out with a boy all the time when he's not into you. I know, I know—you're going to say you're just friends, and it doesn't *mean* anything. Well, you're probably right. It doesn't mean anything to *him*. That's pretty obvious."

"What do you mean?" A wave of annoyance swept through A.A.—what was Ashley suggesting? That she, A.A., was so unattractive that Tri could never fall for her the way he fell for Ashley? That A.A. was into Tri but he wasn't into her?

"*You* know," said Ashley breezily. Tri was ambling back toward them, a bottle of water in each hand. He looked about as happy as A.A. felt, as in not at all. "I better go back in the store before my mother buys some heinous matching bunny rabbit PJs for the entire family. Have fun!"

But fun was the last thing on A.A.'s mind now. The afternoon was ruined.

7

THERE'S A REASON THEY'RE CALLED *SECRET* SOCIETIES

T WAS TOO COLD TO BE STANDING AROUND ON A chilly afternoon outside Nordstrom, but Lauren had no choice. She'd offered to buddy up to the awful Sadie Graham. Make that *re*-buddy up. It wasn't easy. Sadie had totally turned on her after discovering the benefits of her makeover. She had agreed to go shopping that afternoon only as long as Lauren guaranteed that Dex would be there to drive them home later.

Dex was Lauren's good-looking chauffeur and big-brother substitute, not to mention her father's brainy protégé. Sadie had a huge crush on him, Lauren knew. That made Dex her only trump card right now, and she intended to use it—um, him. Dex would be appalled, but her social survival was at stake!

Sadie was making a point by being late. No doubt she and Sheridan were holding their own Congé Committee meeting after school today, delighted to find out they were allowed to take on the Ashleys. Lauren shivered miserably, huddling over her bag, wishing she'd brought gloves. If she dared, she could run inside and buy a pair. But if she wasn't out here when Sadie arrived, the monster-of-her-own-making would probably leave. The only gloves Lauren really needed right now were kid gloves, to handle this whole Sadie situation with care.

Her phone trilled, and Lauren tugged it out of her bag. Sadie ringing to cancel? No, thank God. Someone much more welcome.

"Christian!" she practically shouted.

"Hey! What's up? I'm excused from crew today because my elbow's still strained." Christian had popped his elbow during last weekend's match, which meant they had to call off their ice-skating date later that night and would probably spend the evening playing Monopoly with his mom and stepdad. Not really the romantic evening of holding hands that Lauren had been hoping for. "So, what time are you coming over?"

"Oh! I don't know. I might be late," Lauren told him about meeting up with Sadie at Nordstrom, and how it was a spying mission rather than a shopping trip. He seemed bemused by the whole thing. "I have to get on her good side," she tried to explain.

"Because you want to get into this S. Club thing?"

"S. *Society*. No, I don't want to join them. We want to bring them down."

"We?"

"The Ashleys, of course."

"Of course," he groaned. "I can't keep up with all the politics at your school. Or is it a religion? The Ashleys sounds like a cult to me."

"It is, kind of." She laughed. How annoying that she had to stand around waiting for Sadie rather than go eat frozen yogurt or stroll around the mall with Christian.

"It's just that I hardly ever get to see you." Christian didn't sound too pleased. "If you're not hanging out with your 'Ashleys,' you're planning that Congo thing."

"Congé!"

"And now you're on some kind of spy mission as well. We never get to spend that much time together."

"I want to—you know I want to!" Lauren protested. Shoppers pushed past her, hurrying in and out of Nordstrom's revolving doors. Silently, she was cursing Selfish Sadie. "It's just, things are so crazy right now. And . . . she's here! Christian, I'm really sorry. I have to go. I'll try to be there as soon as I can."

"All right, I'll save Broadway for you. But I can't wait forever," he said, and it sounded like he was annoyed, but Lauren wasn't sure. There wasn't any time to obsess about it now, not with Sadie standing in front of her.

This was the new Sadie—aloof and unsmiling, gazing critically at Lauren with her ice blue contact lenses for eyes. Her hair was a perfect golden blond, shiny and smooth as a helmet. And even though she was in the Miss Gamble's uniform, like Lauren, she looked much more chic than she had a few weeks ago.

She must have taken Lauren's advice about getting it tailored. Lauren had to admit, the outfit did look kind of cute with those long black and gray argyle socks. She'd already heard girls at school talking about Sadie's "signature" look. Ashley Spencer had heard this too: She said the very mention of the words "Sadie" and "signature look" in the same sentence made her throw up a little in her mouth.

"So," said her ex-friend, grimacing at Lauren's YSL bag. "I haven't got much time, you know. I'm really busy right now."

"Planning Congé?" Lauren tried to sound casual. She followed Sadie into the store and up the escalator, waiting for an answer, but Sadie seemed to have gone deaf all of a sudden.

They browsed the 7 for All Mankind and Juicy Couture racks, Sadie complaining the whole time. She preferred J Brand jeans, she said, and Splendid sweatpants, which you could get only at Barneys. No wonder she was busy, Lauren thought: Sadie must be spending all her spare time catching up on her fashion education. A month ago, she didn't know the difference between Anne Klein and Calvin Klein. She thought Dolce & Gabbana were gelato flavors.

"You're so right." Lauren sighed, rifling through a pile of Juicy cashmere sweaters. "These are looking kind of tired."

"I don't know," sniffed Sadie. "I like that gray sweater. It'll look so cute with my socks. They're my signature look, you know."

"Really?" Lauren's face was aching from the strain of her false smile. "Let me get it for you. I was thinking of buying one for myself in green."

"Okay." Sadie sighed, as though she was doing Lauren a big favor by allowing her to buy Sadie a sweater. A really expensive sweater! Lauren picked out two extra smalls and tucked them under her arm.

"You see, in the S. Society," Sadie explained, "we don't believe in wearing matching outfits or carrying matching bags. It's kind of tacky."

"Mmm." Lauren hoped Sadie couldn't hear her grinding her teeth.

"So we have our signature looks." Sadie held up a pair of white Nanette Lepore pants and wrinkled her nose. "I have my socks, and Sheridan has her barrettes, for example. Our new members have to develop their own signature items. That's what the *S* stands for, you know."

"I did not know that," Lauren said. The wide-legged white pants would make Sadie look like a walking fridge, and she couldn't help but hope that Sadie would buy a pair.

"But we also give priority to girls whose names begin with *S*, of course." Suddenly the Queen of Argyle was all chatty. "Supriya Manapali is desperate to join. She's shopping for her signature item today."

"That's great." Lauren felt like she'd run out of inane things to say. "Do you ever go to that boutique on Geary? It's the Ashleys' favorite store."

Sadie's face puckered at the mention of the Ashleys, as though the very idea of them made her physically ill.

"Who cares where they shop? They are old news!" she said, pushing over a tower of BCBG T-shirts and not even noticing. "I'm sick of them running everything. We all are. Why are they always chosen to be models at the Mother-Daughter Fashion Show? Just because Lili's mom is head of the Mothers' Committee!"

"I know." Lauren sighed. It was an open secret that although any girl could be considered for the show, the roster invariably included only the Ashleys and their SOAs, with the Ashleys hogging all the best clothes.

The Mother-Daughter Fashion Show was only fun for the people who were in it. Everyone else always felt like a big, ugly loser. In the past Lauren had usually sat at the same back table with girls like Daria Hart, Guinevere Parker, and Cass Franklin. Girls who would never be picked for the fashion show in a million years. And why not? As Lauren and Sadie had shown, a little makeup and a lot of tan made anyone more attractive.

Lauren suddenly got a brain wave. She *had* to get Daria, Guinevere, and Cass chosen as models for the show somehow. If she really wanted to break the power of cliques in the school, she would have to do more than just sneak into one. She would have to try to encourage real social change. Show them that with the right look and the right opportunity, anyone could be an Ashley.

Of course the Ashleys would protest, but she could make them think it was the S. Society trying to sabotage one of their events.

"Well I'm not going to stand for it anymore," Sadie said, with a toss of her newly golden locks. "At our Congé meeting, I told Miss Charm that the fashion show was just another example of clique dominance at Miss Gamble's, and she totally saw our point. She promised that there are going to be some major changes at the fashion show this year."

"Really," Lauren said. The Ashleys would not like the sound of that. "So . . . what else happened at the meeting?" she asked, pretending to look through a rack of clothes, her heart fluttering.

"We have the best thing ever planned. I'd tell you all about it, but . . ."

"But what?" Lauren was almost breathless with excitement.

"Look at this!" Sadie exclaimed, clutching a bright yellow Rizzo tunic dress. "How cute! Maybe I'll try it on."

"Sure," said Lauren. "But you were about to say—"

"Eek!" Sadie was checking her Rolex. "What time is Dex picking us up?"

"In about fifteen minutes," Lauren said, her heart sinking. "But he won't mind waiting."

"I don't want to keep *him* waiting." Sadie giggled, and Lauren wanted to slap her. If she thought Dex would ever fall for a ninny like her, she was seriously deluded! "Listen, I'll try this dress on while you go buy the sweaters. You know, I'm not sure if I should get a gray sweater or a black one."

"How about both?" Lauren asked wearily. If she could buy Sadie's friendship, maybe then Sadie would talk some more about Congé in the car. And maybe, she thought, stalking over to the cashier's desk, Sadie would end up marrying Dex one day, while pigs flew in the sky over San Francisco Bay.

Whatever the S. Society was planning for Congé, Sadie had no intention of blabbing—not yet, anyway. Lauren would have to come up with a better plan.

8

THE ASHLEYS SHOW
THEIR TRUE COLORS

THAT SATURDAY AFTERNOON ASHLEY sum-
moned the other Ashleys to the elegant Huntingdon
Hotel to get mani-pedis at the Nob Hill Spa, their
current day spa of choice. It was impossible to think clearly
when your nail polish was chipped.

After some deliberation—that is, about five minutes, in
the car on the way to the spa—she'd decided to restrict the
invitation to Ashleys only. Lauren was number three on
Ashley's speed-dial, but just as she was about to press the button, she hesitated.

Sure, Lauren was one of them now—she had the right shoes,
the right bag, even the right boyfriend, but then, it took more
than the right accessories to be an Ashley. It took loyalty.
During the weeks leading up to her birthday party, Lauren had

been hanging out with her old dorky pal Sadie while thinking the Ashleys hadn't noticed. Maybe Lili and A.A. hadn't noticed, but few things escaped Ashley's finely tuned social antenna.

Maybe it was just a coincidence that Sadie had appeared all dolled up and looking like the new *Hills* girl at Ashley's party, but somehow Ashley didn't think so. She thought that maybe Lauren had something to do with it. She didn't know why Lauren would waste her time with such an obvious biter, and she didn't really care to find out.

Ashley had meant what she'd said at the Congé meeting. Unless Lauren proved herself truly worthy of her Ashley affiliation, by infiltrating the pathetic S. Society and uncovering their sure-to-be-sad plans for Congé, she would no longer be one of them.

"I love it here," Ashley said, slipping off her white slippers and plunging her feet into a petal-strewn footbath. They'd all changed into those slippers, and matching white robes, as soon as they'd arrived. Now they were sitting in side-by-side pedicure chairs in an all-white room, waiting to be soaked, exfoliated, massaged, wrapped, filed, buffed, and painted.

"Is this where your mother comes for prenatal yoga?" A.A. asked.

"Ugh. No!"

"Does she go to International Orange? My mother said

they have Mom-to-Be massages there," Lili added.

"You can get that here as well—look." A.A. picked up the menu of services. "The Fifty-Minute Pregnancy Massage."

Ashley screwed up her face. Did they have to keep reminding her that her mother was knocked up? It was bad enough that everyone at Miss Gamble's knew without broadcasting it in public.

And anyway, she had more interesting things to discuss, like her date on Thursday night with Cooper. Her parents felt so guilty about moving her against her will up into the little guest room that they'd allowed her to go out on a date on a school night. It was only pizza again, but the other Ashleys didn't have to know that.

"It was the best date ever," she gushed.

A.A. groaned. "Didn't you already tell us every single detail at lunch yesterday?"

Ashley decided to ignore this. "Really, he's like a male version of me!" She knew that sounded kind of conceited, but she couldn't think of another way to describe it.

"You mean he's got long blond hair and a pet labradoodle?" Lili was in a sarcastic mood—maybe, thought Ashley, because her own life was a boyfriend-free zone. Lili knew full well what Ashley meant: Cooper, like Ashley, was cute and rich.

"You're so funny, Lil." She sighed, splashing her feet in the warm water. "Jealous much?"

"You guys!" A.A. leaned forward. "What we *do* need to discuss is the Mother-Daughter Fashion Show. It's only a week away."

"What's to discuss?" asked Ashley. Talking about Cooper was much more interesting. The Ashleys had always been the stars of the annual Mother-Daughter Fashion Show, which raised money for some sort of charity, and they would be again this year.

Only a handful of mothers and daughters were invited to model in the show. Ashley didn't even care who else got to model, as long as she and her mother got to model the final look, which every year was a pair of white tea dresses. The most beautiful mother-and-daughter duo was always chosen to model those dresses, and for the past two years, Ashley and Matilda had ruled the runway.

"I hope they're going to tell us who's selected on Monday." Lili picked at her fingernails. "I really need to know so I can clear my schedule."

"Of course we'll all be selected!" Ashley didn't know why they were even discussing this.

"Lauren too, probably," A.A. said. "All the teachers know she's in our group now."

"But her mom is such a Donatella," groaned Lili, and A.A. nodded. They all thought, not so secretly, that Lauren's mother, Trudy Page, was kind of tacky and nouveau riche. Trudy was pretty enough, considering she was way old—like, over forty—but she always dressed garishly, in too much Versace and too much bling.

"Where is Lauren?" Lili asked. "Is she not coming?"

"I didn't call her," Ashley said casually. "Sometimes I like when it's just us, you know?"

A.A. and Lili exchanged raised eyebrows, but Ashley decided not to explain further. She had to give Lauren a chance to prove herself. If she delivered the goods, she could remain an Ashley. If not, then best if A.A. and Lili didn't miss her too much.

"I heard Miss Charm telling the headmistress they were expanding the number of girls in the show this year," Lili told them with a frown.

"Oh God, it's probably that S. Society behind it," A.A. said. "They're all over Congé, so it makes sense that they're going to be all over this. We better watch our backs," she said, as she lifted her left foot for the pedicurist to exfoliate.

"Speak of the devil," Ashley muttered, as two familiar-looking girls walked out of the locker room wearing the spa's white robes.

"Oh, look!" said Sadie, in that mocking tone Ashley recognized as her own. "It's the Jonas Sisters!"

"What are you guys doing here?" Ashley snapped.

"This is the S. Society's favorite spa. We like to think of it as the S. Spa." Sheridan sniffed.

"But this is *our* spa." Ashley glared, rising up from her chair a little and getting scolded by the beautician kneeling at her feet for splashing water everywhere.

Sadie folded her arms and sneered. "Funny, because I don't see your names on the front."

Of course, what Ashley meant was that this was the Ashleys' personal spa. Their oasis, their spa-away-from-home.

"What's up with calling yourselves the S. Society, anyway? It's just you and Sheridan. Hardly a society. Not even a group," A.A. pointed out.

"For your information, Supriya Manapali is one of us now, and so is Vicky Cameron," said Sheridan.

"Doesn't everyone have to have a name that starts with *S* for it to be the *S*. Society?" Lili asked.

"For your information, *S* stands for signature. Because we each have a signature accessory."

"I thought the *S* stood for Sucky," Ashley said, disgusted that unwelcome interlopers had crashed their relaxing afternoon.

"What's sucky is your idea for Congé," said Sheridan. "I hear you have nothing."

"That's not true!" Ashley protested, even though it was. Where did they hear that? From Lauren? Lauren wasn't a double agent, was she?

Just then two beauticians called Sadie and Sheridan to their treatments, leaving the Ashleys alone with their thoughts. They all seemed a little shell-shocked by the exchange. No one had ever dared speak to them like that in all their years at Miss Gamble's. It was hard to get used to.

"Ladies, have you all chosen your colors?" asked one of the pedicurists, dipping her hand into each foot basin in turn to check the temperature.

"Yes!" Ashley held up the bottle she'd brought with her, glad to think of something else. She always picked the nail color for everyone, and this one was her particular favorite: Princess Pink. "We'd all like the same thing."

"Actually . . ." Lili looked sheepish. "I'd like to get something different today."

"Er, so would I," said A.A. She pulled a bottle of polish from her pocket and held it up. "I'd rather get a nude shade, so the chips won't show. I always mess my nails up shooting hoops and playing video games."

"And I've brought something new as well." Lili fished in her bag and produced a tiny bottle. "It's called Veruca Violet, and it's totally funky."

"Funky?" Ashley made a face. The polish Lili was brandishing was a deep shade of violet with flecks of silver. "I hope you're not expecting me to wear that."

"No, no," Lili said. "You get Princess Pink. A.A. gets nude, and I get this."

"I don't understand!" protested Ashley. Was the world going mad? "We *always* get the same color."

"Isn't that one of the reasons the S. Society is making fun of us?" A.A. asked. "It's not a bad thing to show people we can think for ourselves. And by the way, what is our idea for Congé? Do we even have one?"

"I agree. It's time we made our own style choices," chimed in Lili. "Ones that reflect our different personalities."

"Fine." Ashley leaned back in her massage chair, trying not to let her annoyance spoil her relaxation time. Let them have their little struggle for independence: This was a battle she could afford to lose. The main thing was to win the war against the S. Society.

"Do you think they have a chance at winning Congé?" Lili asked.

"They're not going to win," A.A. huffed.

"Right," said Ashley, as if the thought had never occurred to her, either. Although inside, her heart was beating rapidly.

The Ashleys simply *had* to win Congé. Otherwise, they might as well transfer schools.

9

LILI TRIES ON OLD CLOTHES
AND PAST LOVES

H**ER VERUCA VIOLET NAIL POLISH STILL** drying on her hands, Lili wandered down the hill to meet her mother. Nancy Khan had an acupuncture appointment that afternoon and had arranged to collect Lili outside the spa at six p.m. Which meant Lili had enough time to wander around the city, walking past some cute stores and doing some window-shopping, while blowing on her daring purple nails.

Near the bottom of the hill, a shop she hadn't noticed before caught her eye. It was called Twist Again, and the sign was as purple and funky as her new nail polish. In the window, headless mannequins modeled amazing outfits.

One was a burnt orange jumpsuit with flared legs that Lili was positive was vintage Halston: She remembered something similar from one of her mother's coffee-table style books. Another mannequin wore the chicest little wrap dress, with knee-high silver boots and gorgeous chunky jewelry.

Lili decided to go in and take a look. She'd never seen anything like those dresses in any other department store or boutique. She'd never been in a thrift store or a vintage store before, mainly because her mother looked down on second-hand stuff, and Chinese superstition said used clothes came with bad karma.

The Ashleys looked askance at the very idea of vintage. A.A. always said she had plenty of new stuff without looking for clothes her grandmother might have worn, while Ashley Spencer sneered that "vintage" was just another word for "trash." These were clothes other people got rid of, she said, because they were old, worn-out, and crummy.

But Twist Again didn't seem like a crummy place. It wasn't down-market or scary. The floors were polished wood, and an iPod station was set up on the counter, playing a song by Cat Power she really liked, one that always reminded her of Max. The friendly assistant smiled at her, explaining how the racks were organized by era, and then left Lili alone to browse. She loved the artwork on the walls, all concert posters from the sixties and seventies; she liked the dressing room curtains, made from hundreds of vinyl records all stapled together. This was such a cool place!

Before long, she was trying on all sorts of interesting clothes: fur-trimmed sweaters, eighties prom dresses, and a dazzling array of Pucci shifts. It was all the kind of stuff she would love to wear, if only she didn't have to look like an Ashley all the time.

But why not wear what she really wanted for once? Loaded down with shopping bags—made, the assistant told her, from recycled lunch bags—Lili staggered up to the front door, pushing it open with her shoulder. The clothes might be a little weird, but she hadn't had so much fun in ages. She had to tell the other Ashleys about this place. Maybe open their minds a bit.

As she walked out, the door almost hit someone waiting to come in.

"Sorry!" she said, looking up with a broad smile. A smile that instantly froze on her face.

Max! He looked as surprised as she felt. The door closed behind them, and there they were, standing on the chilly sidewalk, mouths open like goldfish. Someone had to say something, but what?

"Ah . . . you shop here?" Max finally asked. All Lili could do was nod. She felt completely stupid, as though her head were stuffed with cotton wool.

"It's a cool place." Max said, smiling.

"Yes," she agreed. "It's cool."

There was an awkward silence, and Max looked down at his shoes.

"It's pretty cold today, isn't it?" Lili burbled. She had to say *something*, even if it was completely inane.

"Way colder than yesterday," Max said, and then they fell silent again. Lili's hands were numb and the handles of the bags were digging into her palms, but that was nothing compared with the churning agitation she felt deep inside. Her face was as red as the vintage wrap dress she'd just bought.

"But it was hot in the store," she told him, as though she had to explain away her red face. Why was she acting like such an idiot? Seeing Max turned her brain to Jell-O. He was so cute, with his bright platinum hair and dark eyes. She couldn't help herself: She'd been trying to forget Max, but it was impossible.

Even though he'd been kind of mean to her and had so easily believed all those lies about her, she still really liked him. And he seemed pretty eager to stand around chatting. He could have made his excuses and ducked into the store, but no—he was still here.

"So, do you like it?"

"The store? Yeah. It's, you know, different."

"No, I meant this new sticker." Max was holding up his skateboard and pointing to a wave-shaped blob above the rear wheels. Lili nodded, but she couldn't see anything clearly right now. At least he didn't seem mad at her anymore—that was a relief. Lili had so much she wanted to say to him: that she wasn't lying when she had said she was grounded; that she'd never had another boyfriend, no matter what anyone had told him; and that she'd seen him with another girl who didn't look like she was just a friend.

But how could she just come out and *say* all this stuff when they were talking about a sticker on Max's skateboard?

"I wanted to tell you," she began, trying to get the courage to follow through. "I never dated anyone—"

"Lili!"

Yikes! There was no mistaking that voice. Over Max's shoulder, Lili could see her mother's humungous SUV bearing down on them, its driver's window down. *It's a hybrid!* Lili wanted to tell Max once she saw the disapproving look on his face. He was super eco-friendly, of course.

"Go on. . . . You never dated anyone . . . ," Max prompted.

"I never dated anyone else—," Lili tried to say.

"ASHLEY OLIVIA!"

"I never dated anyone else but you . . . I mean, while we were together. I know someone told you I had been, but it's a total lie. . . . I know you don't believe me, but I couldn't contact you, because I was totally grounded because of the camping trip. My mom took my computer and phone away and everything. . . ."

Max's eyes widened, but before he could respond, Lili's mother yelled again and Lili jumped up, racing to her mother's car.

"Coming, Mom!" she called, trying to pretend that her mother wasn't glaring at them, her face frighteningly stern. Great, now her mother was going to lock her up for the rest of her life.

"Lili . . . ," Max said, trying to catch up with her rapid pace.

But there was no time to hear what he would say, unless she wanted to bring the wrath of Khan down on her head once again. All too soon, Lili and her shopping bags were locked inside, and the SUV was pulling away. She lifted one purple-tipped hand and forlornly waved good-bye. Max raised a hand in return, looking deeply troubled.

Lili consoled herself with the knowledge that even if she'd made a total fool of herself, at least he knew the truth.

10

MEMBERSHIP HAS ITS PRICE

THE ASHLEYS WERE IN CRISIS MODE AND—AS Ashley insisted—something, or someone, had to give. Ashley didn't care that A.A. had to cancel a tennis lesson or that Lili had to give up an afternoon tutoring underprivileged kids. The Ashleys were so busy on Sundays because being fabulous was a 24-hour job. Because if anyone was giving up anything, it wasn't going to be Ashley.

A.A. looked around Lauren's ostentatious house, waiting for the other girls to show, so they could have what Ashley referred to as a Major Brainstorming Session about Congé.

After she rang Lauren's doorbell and was taken aback by its booming chime—based on Big Ben, Lauren explained—A.A. was greeted by Trudy Page.

"I know I should let the butler answer the door," Trudy apologized, ushering A.A. into the concert hall–size lobby, with its pitched glass roof and contorted modern sculptures.

Trudy herself was wearing something semisculptural. It looked like some Alexander McQueen creation that wasn't supposed to be seen anywhere but in a haute couture fashion show or a museum. "But I just get so excited when Lauren has friends over! You're going to have your meeting in the chill-out zone, but until the others get here I thought you could hang out in the game room."

A.A. wasn't surprised that she'd arrived first: Lili was probably racing from the museum, her other Sunday extracurricular, and Ashley was still busy, in all likelihood, supervising the redecoration of her new room. She followed Mrs. Page through a labyrinth of stark corridors and down a flight of stairs into what A.A. guessed must be the game room. Though "room" was an understatement: This was as big as an arena football field, and it looked like one too.

"Is this Astroturf?" A.A. asked, gazing in wonderment at the floor. Trudy beamed, as though she'd just been paid the greatest compliment.

"Looks like it, doesn't it?" she said. "But no, it's Axminster carpet, imported from Devon, England. I got them to custom-dye it so it looks like Astroturf, and then we flew some guys from the NFL over to make sure all the lines were in the right place." Trudy gestured at the yard markers beneath their feet.

"It's pretty amazing," A.A. said, looking around. Sure, it was amazingly tacky, but part of her was drooling over the sixteen-foot screen that took over one entire wall—so perfect for multiplayer zombie killfests.

"Lauren's up in the chill-out zone, but I'll drag her down here. I thought it would be fun for you girls to play with some of our new toys."

A.A. was happy to be left alone. The room was crowded with every possible gadget, from slot machines and arcade games to a neon orange snooker table, a three-lane bowling alley, and a seven-foot animatronic robot marching up and down the sideline. A.A. laughed aloud gleefully, jumping onto an Alpine ski simulator game. The other Ashleys could be as late as they liked: She had a virtual mountain to navigate!

But before she'd finished her third run at the slalom, Lauren appeared, apologizing profusely for her mother's "mistake."

"You weren't even supposed to *see* this room," she said, dragging A.A. by the arm up the stairs. "It's my father's little . . . hobby room. It's a bit too much."

"It's fun!" said A.A., thinking of how much Ned and Tri would love it. She could already picture them riding the mechanical bull set up in one corner and trying to deprogram the robot.

Lauren smiled nervously. "And I'm sorry about my mom nosing around. She really wants to be one of the girls."

"Oh, no worries at all. Your mom's nice." A.A. felt kind of sorry for Lauren. Her own mother, Jeanine, could be embarrassing, but she was never uncool. And Lauren had a lot on her plate right now. If she didn't come up with some inside information on the S. Society, she'd be facing the wrath of Ashley. And *that* A.A. wouldn't wish on anyone.

"About time," Ashley said indignantly when Lauren and A.A. finally reached the chill-out room.

A.A. gazed around the room, understanding at once why Lauren wanted *this* to be their main impression of her house. It was as pristine and white as the spa they'd visited the day before, and the floors were an understated bleached ash. Not a dyed carpet with NFL goal lines in sight.

Lili and Ashley were already positioned in huge, chocolate-colored leather beanbags. Lili looked like she was ready for a nap. Her eyes were red, and A.A. knew she'd been crying all night. Lili had engineered a four-way Ashleys conference call about her disastrous meeting with Max. They all told her she had been right to tell him what she did, and if he didn't believe her, then he wasn't worthy of being her boyfriend anyway. Ashley was sitting up very straight—or as straight as she could manage in a beanbag.

Lauren dragged the remaining two beanbags up so they

formed a circle, and A.A. took her seat. Mmmm, this was comfortable. It was so quiet up here, and just the right temperature. The windows were long, horizontal slits high up in the walls, so all you could see out of them were slivers of sky. No wonder it was called the chill-out zone. And no wonder she was finding it hard to pay attention to Ashley!

". . . squash the S. Society once and for all," Ashley was droning.

A.A. tried not to yawn.

". . . information we need . . ."

". . . doing the best I can . . ." This was Lauren. A.A. pinched herself: She had to stay awake! Lili was practically comatose, and this meeting would be a complete waste of time if they couldn't get any planning done.

"That's not good enough!" Ashley snapped, and A.A.'s eyes popped wide open. Ashley was leaning forward, one accusing finger wagging in Lauren's miserable face. "Don't you understand what's at stake?"

"Really, I do," pleaded Lauren. "It's just taking longer than I thought."

"Maybe if you spent less time thinking about your boyfriend and more time working on Sadie . . ."

"That's not really fair, Ash," interrupted A.A. She couldn't let Ashley get away with this one. All they'd been hearing for the past few weeks was Cooper, Cooper, Cooper!

"Oh, so you're on her side now?" Ashley was obviously in a foul mood. "You don't care if the Ashleys are humiliated?"

"Of course I do!" protested A.A., flopping back into her beanbag. She hated it when Ashley went into attack-dog mode. It was totally counterproductive.

"We all do," chorused Lili, who seemed to have woken from her daze. "But sitting here arguing and making accusations isn't very productive. So I have a suggestion to make. By this time next week, we should all research three ideas. The only rule is—they have to be bigger and better than anything we've done before."

A.A. whistled.

"That's saying something," she said. It really was: Two years ago they'd done the tall-ships tour of the harbor, and last year was the train trip around Napa. And usually they were just competing with themselves for brilliant ideas, not with another rival committee.

"And in the meantime," said Ashley, glowering at the unfortunate Lauren, "one of us has to keep her promise and find out what the members of the S. Society are planning. Or else . . ."

"Or else what?" Lili asked irritably.

A.A. suddenly noticed the unique black-and-white top Lili was wearing. It looked like something from a back-to-the-eighties retrospective on VH1, but in a good way.

"Let's just say we might have to review our *own* membership," muttered Ashley, staring straight at Lauren, who seemed to be cowering in the folds of her beanbag.

It was hard not to feel bad for her. If Ashley wanted Lauren out of the Ashleys . . . well, there wasn't anything in the world that A.A. could do to save her.

11

J. LO IS RIGHT:
LOVE DON'T COST A THING

THE CONGÉ MEETING HAD BEEN AN ENTIRE waste of time, Ashley decided, inadvertently squeezing Cooper's hand with annoyance the next evening. It was another school night, but her parents didn't even notice. They were too busy with the new baby. Cooper squeezed her hand back and grinned at her. They were wandering through Chinatown, strolling up under the ornate Dragon Gate with its stone lions and looking at the cute stuff street vendors were selling. Cooper even bought her the most darling paper fan! He was so cosmopolitan: It was really obvious that he was a world traveler. Every other boy she'd ever known suddenly seemed so provincial by comparison.

If only he would stop saying he "wasn't in relationship

mode." Whatever that meant. He hadn't even wanted to exchange Christmas presents and had forbidden her from getting him anything. Of course she still gave him something—a cozy cashmere scarf monogrammed with his initials. He had yet to wear it, she noticed. She tried to discuss it with A.A., who had been no help, and she tried to ask her father, who just told her she was too young for a relationship and that Cooper seemed like a sensible young man.

But whatever Cooper said, he certainly seemed to like going out with Ashley. As of today, they had been going out for exactly one month and one week. Not that Ashley was keeping count, but . . . she was totally keeping count. Of course! How could she lord it over her boyless friends Lili and A.A. if she didn't keep good personal records of all her romantic triumphs?

One of the things Ashley really liked about Cooper was how creative and imaginative he was. Unlike Tri, for example, who only knew the most *obvious* places on Fillmore, Cooper knew all the coolest spots in San Francisco.

If she'd never met Cooper, Ashley would never have known the museum had a free night. She would never have taken a tour of city hall. She would never have eaten Salvadoran enchiladas in the Mission, or delicious pizza in North Beach's Little Italy. In fact, if Ashley was honest, she didn't even know there *was* such a place as Little Italy, or that they ate enchiladas in El Salvador, until she met Cooper.

"I love the way all the stores are still open at night," she told him, leaning against his shoulder while they peered into a shop selling New Year's decorations. "Is it like this in China?"

"I don't know." Cooper shook his head and looked kind of embarrassed. Cute thing about him Number 106! He was so modest. Not to mention adorably handsome in his beat-up leather jacket.

"I'd love to hear about some of the places you've been," Ashley told him. Maybe with a little bit of encouragement, he'd start opening up.

"Look at that great view of the bridge," he said, turning her around and pointing.

"Can't you see it from your house?" Ashley asked. All they could see from their great room was the bridge. In fact, sometimes it was kind of annoying—it totally blocked the view of Marin.

"I guess. You know, this place is kind of touristy, maybe, but I really like it. There's always something new to see." Cooper tugged her hand, and they moved on. Whenever Ashley tried to ask him about his life, his home, or places he'd been, Cooper just got vague and distant.

"I like new things," she told him, and he seemed to cheer up.

"Really? Even if they're kind of low-key like this?"

"Of course," she told him. "This is my favorite kind of thing to do."

That wasn't entirely true. A mani-pedi, followed by a bout of serious shopping, possibly followed by a professional blow-out and makeup application, and then a huge party somewhere chic—that was really Ashley's favorite kind of thing to do. But this was a very close second.

"I'm glad," Cooper said, his smile sweet and wide. "I'm really glad you're not some pretentious rich kid who only cares about material things."

"God, no!" Ashley shook her head adamantly. She might be rich, but she wasn't pretentious. It was so refreshing that Cooper, Mr. Tycoon, wasn't interested in silly heiresses who wanted to do nothing but party and be superficial. So he didn't like Twenty Questions? That was fine with her. She could just tone it down for a while and focus on enjoying herself. Live in the moment—wasn't that what her dad's Zen Buddhism guru was always going on about?

He was a really nice guy. It wasn't that Tri had been awful—he was fun as well. But Cooper seemed much more into Ashley than Tri ever was. And if she was honest with herself, Ashley had always known deep down, even before he admitted it, that Tri preferred A.A. to her—and that *hurt*.

"That noodle shop I was telling you about is just up here," Cooper was saying, pointing to a narrow staircase across the street. As they wove through the crowd of passersby, Ashley couldn't help noticing a man she'd spotted several times tonight.

He was wearing a dark blue rain jacket, and he was talking into a small headset tucked behind his ear. It seemed like he was always there, wherever they were walking, watching them and muttering into his headset. And wasn't he the guy who'd been sitting at the corner table in the North Beach pizzeria? Weird.

Or not weird at all. Of course! Ashley almost squealed aloud at her own stupidity.

She shouldn't be surprised at all that someone was following them around everywhere. Greek shipping heirs had to protect themselves, obviously. It was probably just Cooper's personal bodyguard.

Ashley shivered with glee. A personal bodyguard! She couldn't wait to tell the other Ashleys.

12

LILI INCURS ASHLEY'S "SIGNATURE" SARCASM

ILI DIDN'T THINK OF HERSELF AS A COWARDLY person, but days were passing and she *still* hadn't made her stand. The S. Society and its idea of a signature accessory were sweeping Miss Gamble's. Daria Hart had started wearing Miu Miu flats personalized with ribbons in Miss Gamble plaid. Catherine Diega flew up and down the hallways trailing a shimmery scarf trimmed with humanely farmed snow rabbit fur and telling everyone her style role model was Isadora Duncan. Whoever that was.

Even Cass Franklin, who couldn't go anywhere without her oxygen tank, had acquired a bejeweled inhaler cozy, which she wore dangling from the strap of her bag. All everyone could talk about was their signature item, and how important it was to develop a unique style.

Finally, on Tuesday morning, when the Ashleys assembled at the Fillmore Starbucks, Lili decided it was time. She arrived promptly, as usual, and ordered her drink before the other girls arrived. Then she dropped her bag on the counter by the window and sat on a tall stool, waiting for all hell to break loose.

Ashley was the last to get there but the first to notice.

"*What* is that?" Ashley pointed an accusing finger at Lili's bag. It was *not* the Ashleys handbag of choice, as Lili knew very well. She lifted her chin in the air defiantly and took a long sip from her hot drink before answering.

"It's a vintage Gucci," Lili said. The bag was a sturdy blue leather in a classic bowling-bag shape.

"Vintage? You mean *secondhand*?"

"I think it's pretty cool," said A.A., stroking the bag as though it were a small pedigreed cat.

"I would totally love one of those!" Lauren enthused. She stared down at her own bag with a look of instant discontent.

"Where did you get it, exactly?" Ashley raised an eyebrow and did not look pleased.

"At this great vintage store in Cow Hollow," Lili told her.

"Ugh!" Ashley wrinkled her nose. "Isn't there a *flea* market down there? Are there going to be *fleas* in this bag?"

Lili rolled her eyes.

"Vintage is all the rage," she informed them. "I think Sophia Loren used to own a bag like this."

"Well, I prefer *Ralph* Lauren," snapped Ashley.

"Pretties, we better go," A.A. interjected. "If we want to get to the bench in time, that is."

Ashley shrugged, prying off the lid of her venti decaf soy latte and blowing on the hot liquid. She was never in any hurry to get to school even these days, even when it was crucial that they arrive before the S. Society.

"Oh . . . the bench." Lauren sighed. Lili knew how she felt. The tussle over possession of the bench outside Miss Gamble's was getting really old, really fast. It made arriving at school every day so tense and nerve-racking. This must be the way every other girl at Miss Gamble's used to feel, walking past the Ashleys every morning! She lowered herself from the stool and picked up her bag.

"Omigod! What happened to your Louboutins?" Ashley shrieked, pointing toward Lili's feet.

"Dude, you're wearing Vans!" Clearly, A.A. couldn't believe it either.

"I thought it was time for a change," Lili said in a low voice. She clicked the soft heels of her black-and-white canvas Vans together. "And these are way more comfortable."

"Comfortable?" Ashley was scandalized. "What do you mean, *comfortable*? What's next? Fat-people jeans?"

"They're cute and all." Lauren was being kind, thank goodness. "But are you sure they'll be allowed at Miss

Gamble's? I thought that saddle shoes were the regulation."

Lili rolled her eyes. She was tired of rules and regulations. She was tired of always being the good girl. She'd never heard from Max after spilling her true confessions to him at the vintage store, and she had to admit to herself finally that he really wasn't interested in her anymore.

Still, the next time she bumped into him, she wanted Max to see the true Lili—not the spoiled rich girl wearing her expensive high heels and driving around in a giant SUV. She wanted him to see the girl who was going to grow up and run a nightclub in New York City. Maybe then he'd realize his mistake. Unlikely, but it was a nice fantasy she harbored.

She liked looking different from the Ashleys for a change. Maybe the S. Society was right on that point— everyone needed their own signature style.

"They make you look short," complained Ashley.

Lili wished Ashley would drop it already. As they approached Miss Gamble's, she saw two girls dashing from a parked silver Lexus SUV toward the stone bench. Sure enough, it was Sadie and Sheridan.

"Quick!" she called to the other Ashleys. "We have to get to the stone bench before they do!"

Lili started sprinting away, glad she was wearing flat shoes for a change, even if they did make her—as Ashley had pointed out—the size of a munchkin.

"Lil!" Ashley called. "No need to run."

"But they'll get there first," Lauren pointed out, breathlessly hustling up. "And I really don't think we should try to drag them off."

None of them were very enthused about Ashley's suggestion last night that they physically remove the S. Society from the bench if they saw them there. Even if it was a four-against-two fight.

"Whatever!" said Ashley breezily. "Just cool it, ladies. Take it from me—there's no need to argue over the bench this morning."

"But they're headed there right now," A.A. pointed out. Sheridan was scampering ahead of Sadie, her Prada coat flapping open. Sadie must have spotted the Ashleys stalking up the hill, because her face was a combination of panic and glee. She was calling something to Sheridan, probably telling her to hurry. They'd be sitting there all gloating and triumphant by the time the Ashleys got there. Lili couldn't stand it.

"Oh God," moaned Lauren. "Shall we just walk past them and go into school early?"

"Go into school *early*?" scoffed Ashley. "I don't think so."

"We could walk behind them and accidentally-on-purpose drip coffee on their heads," A.A. suggested. Ashley sighed, as if this was the lamest idea she'd ever heard.

"Or," Ashley said, "we could just let them sit."

"What?" Lili shot Ashley a look. Was Ashley Spencer actually giving up the fight?

"Let them settle in," said Ashley, smiling in the direction of Sadie and Sheridan. Both were now sitting on the stone bench, with their bags up on the seat as well, so it was impossible for anyone else to squeeze alongside them. Quite a crowd was gathering, as usual these days. All the other girls at Miss Gamble's were loving the Ashleys vs. S. Society showdowns—especially, it seemed to Lili, when the S. Society gained the upper hand. "How long till the bell?"

"Seven minutes," said Lauren, checking the time on her cell phone. She sounded miserable, and Lili wasn't surprised. This was so humiliating!

"Seven minutes—perfect," Ashley said mysteriously. "Just long enough."

"For what?" A.A. asked in a hushed voice. They were approaching the bench, and, Lili guessed, she didn't want Sheridan and Sadie to hear the desperation in her voice. "For us to fight them and get suspended?"

"I don't want to get suspended," Lili whispered. Her parents would kill her, and she'd be off the Honor Board. If they took her BlackBerry away again, how would she ever hear from Max? Not that he'd called her since she saw him at the vintage store, but still . . .

They all stopped in front of the bench. Sheridan and Sadie flashed each other gloating looks. Okay, they'd won. They were Queens of the Bench this morning.

"Morning, ladies!" Ashley called out in a singsong voice. Huh? Why was she acting as though Sheridan and Sadie were her best friends all of a sudden? She addressed Sheridan. "Is that a new coat?"

"It is, actually," Sheridan said. She smoothed down the lapel of her pale yellow coat.

"And Sally—I mean Sadie," Ashley continued. What exactly was she up to? Lili knew Ashley: She had a devious plan. "That is the cutest trench. Is it Dolce? I love winter white, don't you?"

"Duh!" said Sadie. She clearly didn't know what to make of Ashley's compliments either. "I wouldn't be wearing it if I didn't."

"If you're kissing up to us so you'll get an invitation to sit on the bench, you're wasting your time," Sheridan told Ashley. "The S. Society has very high standards. Our members wear signature items. Not matching bags and shoes. Though it looks like Lili's trying to change teams, doesn't it?"

Lili suddenly felt intensely disloyal for bringing a vintage bag to school.

"Thanks," she snapped at Sheridan, "but I don't intend to be on the losing side."

"You're the loser," Sheridan sneered.

"No, *you* are!"

"Wait until Congé's announced," Sadie practically shouted. "Then we'll see who's on the losing side!"

"Now, now," said Ashley, smiling that unfamiliar angel-smile again. "There's no need to shout. You should be enjoying sitting on the bench. It's really quite comfortable, wouldn't you say?"

"Yes, I would say," Sadie replied, not returning Ashley's fake smile. She settled into the bench, leaning her head against the high stone back as though it was a soft, comfy sofa. There must be a method to Ashley's madness, Lili thought, but she couldn't tell what it was yet.

"Could you go stand somewhere else?" Sheridan was waving them away. "All those matching clothes make me feel like I'm in some horror movie where clones have taken over the world."

"You've got some nerve . . . ," A.A. started, one hand balling into a fist.

"No," Sheridan said. "We've got the *bench*. And you haven't. What's wrong, Lauren? Are you tired of being a pseudo-Ashley? Well, too bad. We don't take rejects in the S. Society."

"That's a joke," Lili burst in. How could Ashley just stand there and let them bad-mouth her friends? "You're nothing *but* rejects. That's why none of you would ever be invited to join the Ashleys."

"We wouldn't want to," argued Sadie.

"I just think you're both so brave." Ashley sighed. Everyone looked at her—Sadie and Sheridan, the other Ashleys, and the crowd of delighted, wide-eyed girls crowding the outside stairs. "Wearing such pale colors. I would be worried about sitting . . . well, never mind."

"Sitting where? On the bench? Whatever, Ashley." Sheridan rolled her eyes. "We can sit wherever we like."

"And we like it here," chimed in Sadie.

"Of course you do," cooed Ashley. The bell rang, and all the girls hanging around the stairs sighed—the show was over for another day.

Or was it?

The Ashleys started walking toward the stairs—everyone except Ashley Spencer.

"What are you waiting for?" sniped Sheridan, getting up and grabbing her bag. Sadie stood up as well, tossing her hair and fiddling with the belt of her coat. "Are you waiting until everyone's gone in, just so you can say you got to sit on the bench today?"

"Oh no," said Ashley. "I wouldn't dream of being late for—OH NO!"

Everyone on the stairs stopped dead; girls already inside

the main corridor of Miss Gamble's pushed their way out again, to find out why Ashley Spencer was screaming.

"What?" snapped Sheridan. Lili, who'd had one foot on the bottom step, found herself pushed back onto the sidewalk.

"Your . . . your coats!" Ashley shrieked, then clapped a hand over her mouth, as though she was too shocked to go on.

"What?" Sheridan and Sadie both looked down at their coats, twisting to see the backs. Ashley pointed an accusing finger and gazed up at her audience on the stairs, making sure—Lili was certain—that as many people as possible would look.

"Yuck!" Sadie started battering her coat, frantically dusting off her shoulders and butt. "It won't come off!"

"What won't come . . . OMG!" Sheridan raised one hand: It was covered in thick, ashy dust. She turned around and around in circles, and Lili saw what the problem was. Her entire back looked like it was smudged with charcoal. "My coat!"

"Gosh," said Ashley in a faux-sympathetic voice. Everyone on the stairs was tittering and pointing. "It's not so yellow anymore, is it? That bench must have been *really* dusty."

"You did this!" cried Sadie. Her white coat was a mess. Lili started laughing. Whatever this stuff was, and however Ashley had managed to coat the bench with it, it had certainly done the trick. The queens of the S. Society looked like they'd been climbing up chimneys.

"Did what?" Ashley asked, all innocence. "I don't know what you're talking about. I've been telling the school for weeks that the bench is dirty and needs cleaning. Maybe now they'll do something about it."

"My coat is ruined," spluttered Sheridan.

"You're going to pay for this, Ashley Spencer," Sadie threatened.

"I doubt that," said Ashley. She walked over to Lili and linked arms. A.A. and Lauren, farther up the stairs, smiled down at them. "Maybe you should be more careful where you sit. Just a suggestion!"

"What was that stuff?" Lili whispered when they were safely inside and the giggling masses were dispersing into classrooms.

"It's a charcoal rub you use to clean stone," Ashley confided. "Invisible to the naked eye. You can't buy it in the States—nobody's even heard of it here. Our grounds staff uses it on our fountain. It sits on the stone for twelve hours, and then you have to scrub it off. Otherwise, if you happen to brush against it or sit on it, well . . ."

"You're going to pay for this, Ashley Spencer!" squeaked A.A., imitating Sadie's annoying whine. They all burst out laughing.

"I didn't know what you were up to at first," Lili admitted.

"I thought you might be trying to make friends with them," agreed Lauren.

"Oh ye of little faith," Ashley said, beaming. "Did you really think I'd give up the bench so easily?"

Lili had to hand it to Ashley. Maybe she fought dirty—quite literally—but one thing was sure: On her watch, the Ashleys would *always* come out on top.

13

IS THERE SUCH A THING
AS MOMSWAP?

WHEN **A.A.** GOT BACK TO THE PENT-
house apartment in the Fairmont that
afternoon, her mother was home. This
wouldn't be an unusual event in most households, but
A.A.'s family was not like other families. Most of the time
it was just her and Ned, with a maid or two wandering in
and out.

Their mother, the beautiful former model Jeanine (one
name only), spent most of her time flitting around the
world, falling in and out of love, crashing the front rows at
fashion shows in Milan and Paris, making headlines with her
crazy behavior on yachts in the Caribbean, promoting her
own range of botanical cosmetics on QVC, or sampling new
beauty and body treatments from Bali to Brazil.

Not that she wasn't *there* for her kids: A.A. knew that a quick phone call would bring Jeanine home from wherever she was in the known universe. Jeanine doted on A.A. and Ned. But she was never going to be the apron-wearing, cookie-baking, car-pooling, homework-checking mother A.A. saw on television shows. That was fine with A.A.—who needed a mother in the kitchen when downstairs at the Fairmont there was a team of four French pastry chefs, ready to send up anything A.A. and Ned felt like eating?

But it was still nice to hang out with Jeanine, even if she insisted on redecorating their apartment way too often and kept trying to persuade A.A. to wear high heels and designer clothes when she'd much rather be in yoga pants and a T-shirt.

This afternoon her mother was sprawled on the huge white rug in front of the fireplace, her long legs hoisted straight in the air and her luxuriant dark hair spread out around her. A.A. couldn't tell if she was practicing Pilates or admiring her new shoes.

"Hey, Sporty Spice!" Jeanine called, lowering her legs to the ground.

"Hey, Mom!" A.A. bent over to kiss her mother's forehead and then flopped onto the rug next to her. The roaring fire, controlled—like almost everything in their apartment—by remote control, made the high-ceilinged living room feel warm and cozy.

"Good day at school?"

"It was okay."

"Meet any cute boys?"

"You know that Miss Gamble's is all-girls." A.A. lay back, cradling her head in her hands.

"And that's exactly why I sent you there," said Jeanine. "Keep away from boys, A.A.! That's my motherly advice to you. Listen to the woman who's learned the hard way."

A.A. couldn't help laughing.

"Listen, giggly girl," Jeanine said, sitting up abruptly and shaking her hair. "I got a little favor to ask you. Just a teensy-weensy little favor for your poor old mother."

"What?" A.A. narrowed her eyes. The last time Jeanine asked for a favor, it involved A.A. getting a full preteen botanicals makeover on a stage set up at the mall. The shame!

"You like Marty, don't you?" Jeanine asked. The other week A.A. and Ned had had the pleasure of meeting Jeanine's newest boyfriend. Marty Law was a famous film director who was well known for winning an Oscar for his first and best film, *The Don*, about an Italian mobster family. Since then he'd made a few flops and was now better known for his vineyard in Santa Barbara.

"I guess." A.A. nodded. She'd liked Marty well enough, although she was a little intimidated by his cigar and his bushy silver beard.

"Well," Jeanine continued in her silkiest voice, "he wants to cast you in a movie."

"What?" A.A. sat up, shaking her head in disbelief.

"It's just a small, nonspeaking role," said Jeanine quickly. "And it's only for a few days here and there, filming right here in San Francisco. And there's no problem getting the time off. I've already called what's-her-name at Miss Gamble's. As soon as I told her she'd be invited to the premiere, she was putty in my hands. So what do you say, doll? Isn't it exciting?"

"I guess." A.A. wasn't very enthusiastic. It was bad enough getting her photo taken for those random shoots where Jeanine had to pose as a woman who "had it all," but having a small part in a film probably meant standing around for hours and hours, from dawn until after dark. But her mom seemed super keen on it, and A.A. didn't want to disappoint her.

"Okay, I'll do it. If it makes you happy."

"It makes me very happy." Jeanine beamed. "I'm going to call Marty right away. He'll be more in love with me than he is already. Hey, do you have any idea where that brother of yours is hiding? He's not returning my texts."

"Maybe he's over at Tri's playing a video game," A.A. suggested. "I'll go look for him."

A.A. was secretly pleased for an excuse to go over to Tri's

apartment. They hadn't seen each other for almost a week, since they'd hung out after school riding bikes and bumped into Ashley.

Tri's family owned the Fairmont, so they lived in its other penthouse. Their private elevator opened into a dark lobby furnished with antiques. A beautiful orchid sat in a blue and white china pot on top of a dark, ornately carved table. A.A. pushed open the unlocked front door. She and Ned were welcome at the Fitzpatricks' any time, and they knew the secret elevator code by heart.

There was no sign of the boys inside the apartment—which meant it was quiet, and there weren't pizza boxes and game consoles strewn all over the living room floor. Although this penthouse was similar in size and shape to the Aliotos', it couldn't have been more different in the way it was furnished.

Everything was rumpled and shabby-chic. A leather chesterfield, centered on a big Turkish rug, faced the stone fireplace, and the low tables next to the overstuffed armchairs were piled with books and magazines. A giant French armoire was stuffed full of platters and bowls, with Mrs. Fitzpatrick's extensive cookbook collection jammed along one shelf. A.A. always liked coming here; it felt homey and nice and warm. Plus, it didn't change every other month.

"Hello!" A.A. called, wandering toward the kitchen. Soft

classical music was playing, and she could smell something delicious cooking, like roast chicken.

"In here!" called Mrs. Fitzpatrick. She was standing over their professional-range stove, stirring a bright copper pan of what looked like stock. "Hi, A.A. I'm just thinking about making some soup to have before our chicken tonight. Want to help?"

A.A. agreed, even though she knew even less about cooking than Jeanine. It was always nice hanging out with Mrs. Fitzpatrick—or Supermom, as Ned always called her. Whenever they went over there, she was baking something or planning a family dinner. She was no *Cosmo* cover girl, for sure: She was at least ten years older than Jeanine, at any rate. But this apartment always felt like a home away from home for both the Alioto kids.

Fifteen minutes into stirring together chopped carrots, diced onions, and grated ginger, A.A. heard the front door open and close with a bang.

"Anything to eat?" a familiar voice called. "I can't wait till dinner."

Tri barged into the kitchen, hot and sweaty from crew practice, his dark hair plastered against his face. His blue and gold T-shirt stuck to his chest, showing off his narrow, toned torso. He blushed when he saw A.A., but she tried to focus on stirring the vegetables with a wooden spoon and looking blasé.

But really, her heart was flipping around like a fish out of water. Could it be . . . could it be that she really still liked Tri? That she secretly wanted to be more than just friends?

And, unless her eyes were playing tricks on her, wasn't he looking kind of . . . *tall*?

"You're growing so fast," said Mrs. Fitzpatrick with a sigh, swinging open the tall doors of the full-height pantry and pulling out a Tupperware container. "And eating like it's going out of style. There are crackers here, and you can have some cheese and fruit. And there should be some cookies left from yesterday, unless you've finished them off already."

"I have," Tri said, his mouth already full of crackers, reaching for the jar of peanut butter.

"Aren't you going to say hello to A.A.?" Mrs. Fitzpatrick asked.

"Oh yeah. Hi." Tri didn't even look up at her. A.A. tried not to feel hurt. He just stood there, stuffing his face, ignoring her as though she'd been sent by the caterer to help prepare the meal. Last week they'd had so much fun. Today he was cold and dismissive. What was up with that?

"Would you like something to eat, A.A.?" Mrs. Fitzpatrick asked. "I think I've got some more cookies hidden away."

"It's okay. I should be getting back," A.A. blurted. Her face felt red, either from steam or embarrassment. "I was supposed to be looking for Ned, really."

"I'm going to take a shower," Tri announced, and bounded out of the room without saying good-bye. Mrs. Fitzpatrick shot A.A. a sympathetic smile.

"Are you sure you don't want a cookie?" she asked, and A.A. shook her head. A cookie wasn't going to fix her problems, or make her feel better, even though Mrs. Fitzpatrick's cookies were so good they put Mrs. Field's to shame.

14

THEY'LL ALWAYS HAVE PARIS

THE MONTH OF FEBRUARY ARRIVED, COLD AND gray, but inside the Little Theater at Miss Gamble's, it was springtime in Paris. The Mothers' Committee, which always organized the Mother-Daughter Fashion Show, had done a pretty good job—not that Lili was surprised. Her mother was chair this year of course, as she was every year, and everything her mother accomplished was done to perfection. Nancy "Genghis" Khan used to be a super-lawyer; now she was a super SAHM (socialite-at-home mom). She was used to having everything her way.

Instead of the usual bleachers, clusters of folding chairs and café tables surrounded the temporary catwalk. The stage, banked with long aluminum tubs of yellow roses, was shrouded with pale yellow linen curtains, onto which a silhouette image of the Eiffel Tower was projected. A black wrought-iron pergola in the center of the stage marked the entry point for all the models. The full-length windows along the back wall were draped in back-lit ivory linen, so the room felt like it was flooded with spring light.

On every tabletop a tiny vase held roses of the most delicate yellow; propped against the vases were hand-lettered menus. Audience members could order glasses of champagne or freshly squeezed white peach juice, and waiters in white aprons would bring frosted berries, buttery mini-croissants, and Nutella crepes. Soft accordion music played in the background. The only odd touch was the banner over the main door with the garish YourTV logo plastered all over it—Lauren's father must have sponsored the event. Lili was kind of surprised that Lauren hadn't mentioned it. Maybe she was embarrassed about how tacky it would look. At least nobody would see it until they were leaving.

"It's so beautiful, Mommy!" Lili enthused, clapping her hands with delight. "Everyone's going to love it!" They had arrived there early with the caterers to supervise setup.

"I'm glad you approve," said Nancy, smiling. They'd declared a truce this week: Lili had promised to focus on her schoolwork and other activities, and Nancy had promised not to freak out if Lili was five minutes late getting to the car or the dinner table.

Lili suspected her mother secretly approved of her new vintage look—not because Nancy approved of buying second-hand clothes, but because she always liked it when Lili emerged a little from the shadow of Ashley Spencer.

"Models! Backstage, please!" Vicky Cameron's mother, a member of the Mothers' Committee, rushed at them, waving her clipboard and gesturing to the door alongside the stage. "The audience will be arriving soon!"

"Of course," said Nancy, steering Lili toward the stage door. "I hope all the clothes have been arranged as I instructed. One rack per each mother-daughter team, each clearly labeled!"

The racks were labeled, just as Nancy had arranged, but backstage was still a scene of total chaos. The place was packed with mothers and daughters, along with their personal hair-stylists and makeup artists, plus photographers they'd engaged to document every loving family moment.

Some unscrupulous mothers were raiding other racks, grabbing cuter outfits and pilfering accessories. Yikes! Lili hoped no fights would break out. Last year, when the theme was Pastel Parade, two of the mothers got into a major slap-down over a mauve, pearl-fringed cashmere wrap with matching Jimmy Choos. This being San Francisco society, no physical harm had been inflicted, of course, but there were a lot of frosty glares and hard feelings.

"Lili!" Ashley was waving frantically from a relatively peaceful corner. She and her mother, Matilda, were already dressed in their first outfits, elegant Diane von Furstenberg tie-front dresses, their golden hair loose and shining. "We've roped this area off."

Lili had to hand it to Ashley: She was a mistress of crowd control. She and Matilda had brought the red velvet rope last seen at Ashley's birthday party and had used it to cordon off a little insanity-free zone in one corner. A.A.'s rack was there as well, but there was no sign of A.A. or her mom yet. Lauren's rack, Lili noticed, was pulled alongside the rope— but not *inside* the inner sanctum. Interesting.

"How are you feeling?" Nancy asked Matilda Spencer, resting a sympathetic hand on her arm. "Are you over the first-trimester nausea?"

"Not yet, unfortunately." Matilda nodded.

"She's already puked twice this morning," Ashley whispered to Lili. "If she pukes on the runway, I'll have to leave the state."

"Hello, hello! May we join you?" Uh-oh. That piercing voice. That overpowering smell of Poison by Christian Dior. That eye-crossing excess of zebra print from her tacky floor-length coat. The blinding flash of yellow gold jewelry. It *had* to be Lauren's mother.

"Of course!" said Matilda, though Lili could swear she

saw Ashley's mom exchange a quick smile with Nancy. "They've asked us to try on all our dresses before the show begins, just to make sure everything fits."

"But Trudy, I thought you didn't approve of fashion shows," Nancy remarked.

"Oh no! It's beauty pageants I don't like," Trudy shouted, unwinding what looked like a six-foot-long python from her neck. Lili was relieved to see it was only a scarf with a snakeskin pattern. "Fashion is different. And of course I couldn't disappoint Lauren. She's been looking forward to this for weeks!"

Lauren didn't look like she was looking forward to anything. Lili thought she looked pretty upset when she noticed that their rack hadn't been placed inside the Ashleys' sanctum, and she kept glancing around the crowded room, not paying attention while her mother jangled her bracelets and gabbed on about the cute Michael Kors silk halters Lili and her mom were going to wear as their first look.

While Lili slipped out of her shoes, hanging on to the rack to keep steady, she glanced around the room as well. When the announcements had been made, the Ashleys had been irritated, but not too surprised, to hear that the odious girls from the S. Society had been chosen to model too. The weeks leading up to the fashion show had been frosty between the two camps.

Sheridan Riley's spindly legged, redheaded mother looked terrified to be there, almost shivering in her strapless Nicole Miller number. Sheridan, however, was beaming around the room, her pointy nose stuck high in the air. Ugh.

Even more annoying, that worm Sadie Graham and her mother had set up camp right by the Ashleys' enclosure. Every five seconds Sadie was looking over at the Ashleys' clothing racks, as though she had her eye on something. *Watch your step!* Lili wanted to tell her. There was no way she was getting her hands on any of their stuff. Where were all her *signature items* now, huh?

Lili stood up, pulling the Michael Kors dress over her silk camisole and boy-short pants, making sure it was a perfect fit. Not bad at all! This fashion show was going to be amazing, even if the losers from the S. Society had managed to wriggle their way in. At least the audience would be able to do a quick compare and contrast: Ashleys versus Pretenders. Who would come out on top? Lili thought there would be no contest whatsoever.

Plus, how three of the nerdiest loser girls in school had been chosen to model at the Mother-Daughter Fashion Show, the school's prime beautiful-people-only event, Lili had no idea. The news had been downright shocking when it was announced at MODs last week. Maybe Ashley was right: All this anticlique lobbying done by the S. Society—in order to grab Congé off its rightful owners, the Ashleys—was ruining the school. If just *anyone* could model in the fashion show, what was the point of taking part?

There they were now: Droopy little Daria Hart. Guinevere "Bobblehead" Parker, whose knobbly knees were bigger than her bustline. Cass Franklin, with her oxygen tent, mouth-breathing at the sight of her clothes rack.

Hang on, was Lauren actually sneaking over there to talk to them?

15

SHE'S NOT FAT,
SHE'S MY MOTHER

ASHLEY SIGHED LOUDLY WHILE SHE TIED her dress around her waist. It was bad enough that she had a mother running to the bathroom every ten minutes to throw up her organic oatmeal and prenatal-vitamin-supplemented juice smoothie, but it was even worse to congratulate yourself on being part of a supposedly elite group only to realize that the inmates had taken over the asylum.

Ashley knew they were going to be there, but she hadn't realized the extent of the fashion-tragedy-in-the-making until she saw them in the flesh.

What was the model selection committee *on* when they let in Guinevere Parker and her matching mousy mom? Or Daria Hart and her drowned rat of a mother? And

Cass Franklin—really! Whose idea of a joke was that?

And now, just to make everything even more insufferable, Sadie Graham was leaning against the red velvet rope (designed to keep plebes *out* of the Ashleys' enclosure). Even the jaunty Tocca dress and that cute pair of Missoni sandals she was wearing couldn't disguise the fact that Sadie would never, ever be welcomed into the Ashleys' fold.

And look at her now—she was actually reaching out and *touching* something. On. Ashley's. Rack. OMG! Ashley was going to have her arrested, then expelled, and then banned from the entire Pacific time zone.

"What do you think you're doing?" she demanded, pouncing out from behind A.A.'s untouched rack of clothes. (Where *was* that girl, by the way?)

The unbearable Sadie didn't even have the grace to look startled, let alone guilty.

"The Mothers' Committee has informed me that *we*," she said, gesturing at her simpering mother, "will be wearing the white tea dresses this year."

"As if!" Ashley snorted. Matilda was in one of the dressing rooms at this very moment, trying on her white dress.

"I can only see one dress," Sadie persisted. "And it should be on *our* rack, not yours."

"You're totally misinformed." Ashley grabbed the rack and wrenched it away from Sadie's sweaty-palmed grip.

"*We're* the ones wearing the white dresses, as usual!"

"Really?" One of Sadie's perfectly arched eyebrows shot up. "Are you sure?"

Ashley heaved the most melodramatic sigh she could muster without hyperventilating. Of course she and her mother, as the most beautiful mother-daughter team, would once again be modeling the final look of the show.

"Just go back to your . . ." Ashley fluttered a dismissive hand in the direction of Sadie's section. "Your little side of the room, okay?"

"Sweetie, what do you think?" Matilda had emerged from her dressing room, draped in the bias-cut ivory J. Mendel gown. Her beautiful face looked wan and worried, and she had pulled her long hair back with one hand.

Yikes! The dress was way too clingy, and Matilda's baby bump was totally showing.

"Your mother is too fat for that dress," Sadie hissed, so only Ashley could hear.

"She's not fat," Ashley spat back. "She's pregnant, you moron!"

"Matilda, you look lovely," Sadie's mother cooed sweetly. "Like a shotgun bride." Her smile was acid as she looked her up and down.

"You know," Matilda said, tugging at the dress, "I don't think the fit is very good."

"That bias cut is very unforgiving," Sadie's mother agreed. "It shows everything, doesn't it?"

"And I have a little too much to show right now." Matilda sounded rueful, but not too upset. "Oh well! Someone else should wear the white dresses this year."

"Mom!" Ashley was outraged. Her mother was giving in way too easily. She could carry a bouquet of flowers or a basket of something. Then nobody in the audience would notice a little bump. After all, her mother was pregnant in the way celebrities were pregnant—with stick-figure arms and toned legs and just a teeny basketball where her waist used to be. Thankfully Matilda hadn't puffed out like a pregnant piñata. Ashley was spared at least *that* shame.

"Ashley, I'm kind of tired." Matilda was already pulling at the dress, getting ready to slip it over her head. "I think three changes of clothes is plenty for me right now. Let someone else wear the dresses. I think Sadie and her mother would make a beautiful finale."

"Thanks, Mrs. Spencer!" Sadie practically shrieked. Ashley felt her face burning. If she and Matilda couldn't wear the white dresses, then at least the honor should go to one of the other Ashleys. But Sadie had already grabbed Ashley's dress off the rack, and Matilda was passing her dress across the red velvet rope to Sadie's mother. All was lost!

"What's going on?" Lili bounded up, wearing the cutest gingham Marc Jacobs frock.

"Where've you been? And where is A.A.?" Ashley fumed. "I'm under attack here, and I have *no help whatsoever.*"

"You're not wearing the white dresses?" An aghast Lili was looking over at Sadie and her stick-insect mother.

"No." Ashley folded her arms and stamped one foot on the ground. "There's no point in doing this stupid fashion show at all."

Matilda, swaddled in a soft cotton robe, leaned over and tapped Ashley on the arm.

"We'll have none of that, thank you, Ashley," she said, her blue eyes steely. "This show is for charity, remember? It's not about who wears the most dresses. Now go and finish putting on your shoes for the first outfit. No, not another word!"

Ashley reached for Lili's hand and dragged her to the corner. She wanted to sit someplace the awful Sadie Graham couldn't see her—and where she couldn't see Sadie Graham.

Her mom was deluding herself if she thought this fashion show wasn't about who got to wear the most dresses. *Life* was about who got to wear the most dresses! Matilda was living in a bubble. Having this baby had made her mind go foggy.

"Don't worry." Lili squeezed Ashley's hand. "We'll pay Sadie back somehow."

Ashley sniffed. The only thing that would make her feel better now was Sadie falling off the runway, or possibly the whole show being canceled. At least she had Lili here to comfort her. But where had Lauren wandered off to? And where on earth was A.A.?

16

LITTLE MISS HELPFUL
IS ANYTHING BUT

Ouch! You're pinching me!"

Lauren was pinning the back of Guinevere Parker's boxy Phillip Lim dress, so it didn't hang from her body like a shapeless sack, but all Guinevere could do was complain.

"I thought you were supposed to be helping *me*," whined Daria Hart. She was stuck halfway in a ruched Tibi sundress, because—as Lauren could see quite clearly—Daria had failed to notice the side zipper.

"I don't like any of these things," moaned Cass Franklin, her oxygen tank bashing the back of Lauren's head. "I don't think I want to do this show after all. Where's my mom?"

Lauren gritted her teeth and kept pinning the back seam of Guinevere's dress. What a bunch of divas! These girls weren't grateful at all that Lauren—or rather, Lauren's father's money—had secured them a place in the fashion show. Of course, they had no idea Lauren was behind it, but it still annoyed her that all they could do was complain and pout. They were even worse than the Ashleys. At least the Ashleys knew how to dress themselves. Lauren herself was wearing an adorable Foley + Corinna maxi dress that showed off her delicate collarbone nicely. She was excited to be part of the fashion show at last and a bit irritated that she was spending it with the moaning Myrtles.

Last night had been so much more relaxing. She and Christian had gone to an early movie and then hung out for a while in a cute little café on Union Square, with armchairs in the windows, Latin lounge on the stereo, and Moroccan tea lights on every table. They'd sat huddled in the corner, sharing a giant piece of blueberry cheesecake and fork-fighting over the final blueberry. Christian let her win with a smile. Lauren wished every day was that stress free.

She felt a little bad for boring Christian by talking incessantly about everything that was happening at school. Christian had tried to be interested and concerned, but he was a boy, after all—he wasn't used to so much drama. Boys were really different. If they didn't like someone, they just steered clear of them, or kept it to themselves. They didn't have major cliques fighting for control of their schools or dictating what everybody wore. Talk about a different way of life!

She took a quick glance toward the Ashleys' corner. Lauren had snuck away when Ashley and Sadie were having the tug-of-war with the white dresses, and Lili had been busy placating her mom because the chocolate Eiffel Tower miniatures were melting under the heat of the lights. Lauren wanted to check on the three girls out of kindness, to see if they needed any help, since they were new to the event. But they'd taken her offer as an opportunity to treat her like a servant, and Lauren felt a little bit like Cinderella sur-rounded by her stepsisters.

"Now it's too tight," Guinevere bleated, pointing at her skinny, bobbleheaded reflection in one of the tall mirrors propped around the walls.

"Stand still, Daria!" said Lauren as she wrenched the zip-per down.

"This is way too itchy!" Daria lamented. She picked at the dress gingerly, as though it were made out of steel wool. "It's digging into me everywhere. Mom! Mom! Where is she?"

"Probably hiding in the bathroom," muttered Lauren. Really! You'd think this fashion show was a punishment rather than a special treat. Did these guys have any idea how hard she'd had to work to get them in here at all?

If Lauren hadn't argued and lobbied on their behalf—

not to mention persuaded her father to write Miss Gamble's a Very Big Check—then they'd all be sitting in the audience right now, chewing their cuticles and getting bits of fruit stuck in their braces.

"And I don't know what I'm supposed to do with this." Cass was still moaning away, leaning on the clothes rack as though it were a Zimmer frame. Lauren glanced up, already exhausted.

Cass clutched at her oxygen tank. What was she doing? Trying to tuck it into the belt of her Daryl K dress? Stuffing it into a pocket? Whatever she did, it was going to ruin the line of the dress.

"Can't you leave that thing backstage while you walk down the runway?" Lauren asked, her voice revealing the strain. She didn't want to be here, helping these three ungrateful wretches.

She wished she were hanging out with the Ashleys, trying on clothes, making sure her mom didn't say anything too embarrassing to the other moms, having fun behind the red velvet rope—or standing next to it. She didn't quite believe Ashley's excuse that there was "too little space" in her makeshift enclosure. Instead she was crawling around on her hands and knees, hoping the Ashleys wouldn't spot her, while the very people she was trying to help treated her like dirt.

Lauren had thought she was doing a good deed by breaking

the Ashleys' iron grip on the Mother-Daughter Fashion Show, but obviously she was as wrong as that coat her mother was wearing.

Doing good meant nothing if the recipients of her magnificent charity didn't want it. These girls would be so much happier, she decided, if they were just left to sit in the back as usual. They didn't know how to be the center of attention. They just felt uncomfortable and self-conscious.

"I think I feel an attack coming on," Cass wheezed, and Guinevere started frantically fanning her with a Chloé clutch purse.

"I can't breathe either," said Daria. "And I can't walk in these shoes."

"Neither can I!" Guinevere commiserated, dropping the clutch purse onto Lauren's foot. "And you know my mother? She needs orthopedic insoles, otherwise she strains her knees. She'll just have to wear Birkenstocks with her dresses."

Lauren gulped, trying not to lose her temper. Were these girls crazy? Or maybe *she* was the crazy one. What was it her father always said? The road to hell is paved with good intentions.

But then, just as Lauren was going to write them off entirely, Guinevere started to laugh—a clear, joyful laugh, full of delight because she'd just seen herself in the mirror. Then Daria started to laugh too, and so did Cass.

"We look good!" Cass marveled. "Wow."

"I know!" Daria agreed, looking breathless. "I didn't think it was going to be possible!" And suddenly Lauren understood why they had been so difficult earlier. They had been nervous about being exposed as freaks who had no business walking down the Mother-Daughter runway. They were trying to appear like they didn't care about the event because in reality, they cared way too much.

"Thanks, Lauren," Guinevere said. "We know it was you who got us in."

"I didn't do anything. . . ." Lauren shrugged, smiling at the three of them. They did look awesome, like a certain trio of pretty girls who were laughing and enjoying themselves for being in the right place at the right time.

Lauren was just glad to be proven right. Anyone could be as pretty and fabulous as the Ashleys. All a girl needed was a chance to shine.

17

SUPERMOTHER RULES
THE CATWALK

A.A. WAS NOT ASHLEY—AND THAT MEANT she hated being late.

By the time she and Jeanine arrived at the Mother-Daughter Fashion Show, everyone was already dressed, and a member of the Mothers' Committee was lining them all up for the first walk down the runway.

"Where have you been?" asked Lili, tugging A.A.'s first outfit off its hanger and handing it to her.

"You almost missed me." Ashley dabbed at invisible tears with a scarf she'd purloined from Sadie Graham's clothes rack. "I very nearly walked out. I only stayed for my mother's sake. She looks forward to this lame event way more than I do."

"Don't talk to me about mothers," A.A. shot back quietly,

trying not to pull away when Lili climbed on a chair and started fixing her hair. "*My* mother can barely remember to come home, let alone get herself anywhere I want to go on time!"

Jeanine was notorious for disappearing when she had a new boyfriend, and this week was no exception. All week she'd been holed up in Ibiza—which apparently was some glamorous Spanish island in the Mediterranean, where there were nightclubs lining the streets and everyone was tanned and fabulous—with her new boyfriend. (Not some gorgeous Spanish guy either, A.A. told her friends. It was just Marty, the film director guy with the big Santa Claus beard. She was surprised old guys like him were even *allowed* on Ibiza.)

A.A. had texted Jeanine about the fashion show every day to remind her. Her mother had promised faithfully that she'd be there on Sunday, but somehow she'd managed to forget. She'd only just arrived from the airport!

A.A. had been sitting in the apartment all morning, not knowing whether her mother would make it back on time. They'd had to hustle to get to Miss Gamble's, and Jeanine was a wreck—yawning every two minutes, her Jackie O shades hiding the shadows under her eyes.

"Jeez, does your mom know this show is about Paris in the spring—not rehab in Colorado?" Ashley muttered, dabbing blush onto A.A.'s pale face.

"I know she looks bad," A.A. shot back quietly. "Even

worse, she just keeps going on about how much in love she is."

"Ew!" chorused Lili and Ashley. Nobody wanted to hear about old people falling in love. It was gross and probably illegal.

"She's even talking about getting married again," whispered A.A., cramming on a chunky Lucite bracelet.

"I love Paris in the springtime!" Jeanine sang in a throaty voice, ruffling her luxuriant mop of dark hair. She was at the other end of the rack, already wearing the slinky jersey dress that hugged her every curve. She'd stripped down and dressed up in two seconds flat.

That was the good thing about being a former model, A.A. guessed—you mastered that whole quick-change artist thing. The bad thing, however, was that her mother applied the quick-change philosophy to nearly every aspect of her life. Home decor, vacation destination, and—most of all—men.

"She totally forgot about the brunch," A.A. told the others, her voice low and angry. She hated it when her mother didn't remember stuff in her own daughter's life. Every time Jeanine met a new guy, she forgot all about her kids.

"The main thing is, she's here now," Lili reassured her. A.A. couldn't even muster a smile. Lili's mother never forgot *anything*. She might be bossy and stern, but she really cared about Lili.

Ashley's mother was devoted to her, too, however much Ashley thought she was neglected and overlooked. Even Lauren's brassy mother—who looked kind of tasteful, for once, in her first outfit, a beige Chanel suit picked out by the Mothers' Committee—was always coming up with ways to make their home more fun and comfortable for her family. What did Jeanine do? Run off with weird old guys and party like it's 1989.

"Ladies!" shrieked the committeewoman with the clipboard. A.A. could hear the music in the auditorium swelling—it was some old recording of a creaky-voiced French dude singing "Thank Heaven for Little Girls." "We're ready for our first mother-daughter pair! Everyone in line, chop-chop!"

"Chops!" groaned Jeanine, pulling her skirt up so it was about three inches higher than it should be. "That just reminded me—I'm starving! Do they have anything to eat around here? Champagne? Caviar?" She looked around hopefully.

"Mom, this isn't Fashion Week. You should have come home earlier if you wanted to eat!" A.A. dragged Jeanine next to her at the end of the line.

"I can't make the plane fly any faster," Jeanine protested. She ripped off her dark glasses and tossed them aside.

"Could you look any more sleep deprived?" grumbled

A.A. She might not be obsessed with this fashion show the way Ashley was, but she didn't want to make a fool of herself. Or have her mother stumble down the runway looking dazed and confused.

"What are you worried about?" Jeanine seemed to read her thoughts. "I'm a professional, remember? I can walk down this runway with my eyes closed. We'll kick the rest of those mother-daughter butts. But first, missy, you better put on your shoes."

A.A. bent down to wind the straps around her ankles, but something was wrong: The long strap on the left shoe was fine, but the strap on the right shoe was much shorter, as though someone had bitten it off. The sandal wouldn't stay on A.A.'s long foot without its strap.

"Huh?" she mumbled, fidgeting with the strap. She looked up at her mother. "This is broken."

"Quick, grab another pair," ordered Jeanine. A.A. raced over to their dressing area, leaping over the red velvet rope. What else would go with this dress—the striped wedge espadrilles, maybe? Here was one of them, but where was the other? A.A. tore through the pile of shoes under her rack, but the second shoe was nowhere to be found.

"A.A.!" Her mother sounded agitated. "We're on in two, babe."

A.A. decided to grab any pair at all and wear them—as

long as the shoes had heels, they'd look okay. But half of her shoes seemed to be AWOL. And the ones that *were* there were all damaged in some way—straps severed, heels snapped off. One pair of jeweled mules had been cut so when A.A. slid her feet into them, they simply fell off, dropping to the ground with a metallic thud. WTF? Who had sabotaged all her shoes?

There was no point in grabbing a pair assigned to one of the other Ashleys—Lili's feet were tiny, and Ashley and Lauren wore size sevens, not A.A.'s giant elevens. The only person she could borrow from was her mother. A.A. reached into Jeanine's pile of shoes, pulling out a pair of Manolos. Thank God! But wait a second—one of them had no heel. Or rather, the heel had been pulled off. Jeanine was wearing her own shoes for the first walk, so she hadn't had time to notice that the rest of *her* shoes had been sabotaged as well.

"All our shoes are busted," A.A. told her mother, rejoining her in the line. Her heart was pounding. Why didn't the stupid S. Society take their revenge on Ashley Spencer? This was what A.A. got for having enormous feet, she guessed—she was the easiest target. They must have known she and Jeanine wouldn't be able to borrow shoes from anyone else there. "All of them are slashed or messed up or broken or one of a pair is missing. Someone must have done this to stop me from walking in the show."

"Some jealous loser," said Jeanine, who didn't seem at all surprised. "It used to happen all the time in Milan. Where are the shoes you wore here?"

"Running shoes." A.A. made a face, and so did Jeanine.

"There's only one thing we can do," her mother said, pulling off her heels. "And that's to go barefoot."

"With every outfit?"

"Why not? We're tall and gorgeous—we can carry it off. And what's the alternative? Drop out of the show? That's what the bitches want. One year they stole mine and Cindy Crawford's swimsuits during the *Sports Illustrated* shoot! But that didn't stop us—we started the trend of painting them on. Talk about sexy." Jeanine winked.

"A.A. and Jeanine—you're on," said the mother with the clipboard. "Where are your shoes?"

"We don't need shoes," said Jeanine, taking A.A.'s hand and squeezing it tight. "We're the Amazon Aliotos. We're fierce!"

In spite of everything—her nerves, her anger, her disbelief that someone would pull this stunt on her—A.A. couldn't help smiling. Her mother was unconventional, and that was one big pain in the neck most of the time. But for once A.A. was ready to forgive Jeanine for being *so* late and *so* selfish and *so* in love with some old guy from L.A. who wasn't even cute or famous, because she had to admit one thing: Her mother was right.

They were the Amazon Aliotos. When Jeanine stomped out, knees high, arms swinging, she looked every bit as good as she did in 1989, when designers paid her hundreds of thousands of dollars to show off their clothes.

A.A. figured that was why they called them supermodels. They had the superhuman ability to make anything look good. It would take a lot more than a few stolen shoes to keep them from *owning* that catwalk.

18

LAUREN WAVES
THE WHITE FLAG

THE SABOTAGE AT THE MOTHER-DAUGHTER Fashion Show had brought everything to a head—or maybe a boil—between the S. Society and the Ashleys. Because the Ashleys had "ruined" Sheridan and Sadie's coats, A.A.'s shoes for the fashion show had been "ruined" right back. The past month had been a chaotic and unpredictable one. You never knew what would happen next. The other week Sadie had "accidentally" thrown paint on Ashley's school uniform during art class, and yesterday Lili had opened her handbag at lunch to discover it had been infested by ladybugs.

The Ashleys never took any of this lying down, and Ashley vowed revenge on every new trick. At least the stone bench had been out-of-bounds for a while, cordoned off until the contractors hired by Miss Gamble's to scour it clean could finish their work.

Lauren couldn't help but feel kind of responsible for all this animosity. If she hadn't upset the natural order of things at Miss Gamble's, then nobody would be destroying one another's things with such vengeful glee. The Ashleys would still be sitting on the bench every morning, Sheridan would still be waving to them on her way into school, and Sadie would be practically invisible, not really caring whether the Ashleys liked her or not. But instead, everyone was in a state of near hysteria, planning the next evil attack. No one was safe.

It had gone on long enough. Lauren sent out a text message at break. She sent the same message to all the Ashleys, and to Sheridan and Sadie. It read: WAR TALKS @ 12, LIBRY, NO WEAPONS!

After honors history, she raced along the polished wooden corridors to the heavy oak doors of the library. She attached a handwritten sign to the door (CONGÉ COMMITTEE MEMBERS ONLY) and slipped into place at the head of the table. Lili was the first to arrive, of course.

"What's all this about?" Lili asked, sliding a pile of books onto the broad table. "Did Ashley approve this meeting?"

"I most certainly did not." Ashley swept in and sat down next to Lili. Lauren gulped: Ashley might be furious about this. But actually, she didn't seem that mad. She looked as worn out as Lauren felt, as though all this conniving was starting to take its toll.

A.A. arrived a minute later, chomping on an apple, and then, at 12:05, Sheridan and Sadie walked in together. They were holding their heads high, looking as snooty and pained as usual, but Lauren could tell they were nervous. After all, there were only two of them. The four Ashleys might be planning to lock the door and pummel them into submission with dusty volumes, or leave them tied up with pantyhose and hanging from the chandelier.

"Thanks, everyone, for coming today," said Lauren, when the S. Society had taken seats opposite the Ashleys. "Please listen to what I have to say. Congé is just a couple of weeks away. We all need to focus if we're going to come up with brilliant ideas."

"Who says we don't have a brilliant idea already?" sniped Sheridan.

"Uh . . . let me think," retorted Ashley. "The fact that you're stupid?"

"You're the one to talk!" Sheridan looked outraged.

"Please!" Lauren held up a hand. "I've asked you to hear me out. We're ALL working on Congé right now. We need to make it a success—whoever wins. Because if we don't, then the teachers might decide to create an entirely new committee next year, and *none of us* will be on it."

She paused, gazing around the five faces at the table. All of them seemed to register the horror and disgrace of being ousted from Congé insider status.

"So what are you suggesting?" A.A. asked, licking apple juice off her fingers. "That we work together?"

"Never!" shouted Sheridan.

"As if!" Ashley rolled her eyes.

"No, I'm not suggesting that," said Lauren, trying not to raise her voice. She had to keep her head. "What I'm proposing is this. We all leave each other alone until after the successful Congé bid is announced. No more pranks. No more sabotage."

"I have no idea what you're talking about," said Ashley.

"But *they* do," said Lili accusingly, glaring at Sheridan and Sadie.

"Don't act all innocent with us!" Sadie looked outraged. "My coat's only good for a dog blanket now!"

"Well, as you're a *dog*—," Lili began, but Lauren cut her off.

"No more fighting!" she ordered. "Let Congé decide. Whoever wins Congé wins the bench. Simple as that."

"What?" Sadie didn't seem to understand.

"Are you saying we might have to give up our right to the bench?" A.A. asked.

"It's not your right," fumed Sheridan.

"Whatever! As if *you* have any right—"

"Oh, we're talking about *rights* now, are we? Since when do the Ashleys care about anyone having rights?"

Lauren gripped the edge of the table. This wasn't working. It was a good idea, but they were all too competitive and irrational. Oh well—at least she'd tried.

"I understand," said Ashley in a quiet voice. She gave an expert flick of her golden blond ponytail. "I think it's a good idea. Whoever wins Congé wins the bench. Simple. Let's do it."

"Really?" Lauren couldn't believe it.

"Sure." Ashley crossed her arms.

Sadie smirked. "I've got a better idea. Want to make it interesting? Let's agree that whoever wins Congé wins it all. The bench. The table in the refectory that's nearest the window. Social Club."

Ashley frowned. Sadie had just put more things into play. The Ashleys' table at the ref was hallowed ground, and so was Social Club—it was the only after-school activity that included the possibility of meeting boys from Gregory Hall. The Ashleys ran it as their private domain.

She looked like she was going to argue, but in the end, she merely shrugged. "Sure. Why not?"

"You're awfully confident about winning Congé," Sadie said.

"That's right."

"Well, maybe you shouldn't be."

"Maybe. Maybe not."

"If Ashley thinks it's a good idea, then so do I." A.A. sighed, dumping her gnawed apple core on the table. "Let's do it."

"Okay," agreed Lili. "We're going to win, so . . . why not?"

"I think you'll find *we're* going to win," Sheridan insisted.

"So it's agreed?" asked Lauren.

"How do we know you'll keep your word?" Sadie challenged.

Ashley rolled her eyes. "Do you really think we would welsh on a bet? Get serious."

"We would never do that," Lili stated.

"That's, like, so low," A.A. chimed in.

Finally Sadie and Sheridan seemed satisfied. The bet was on. Lauren exhaled a sigh of relief.

For now at least, she had brokered peace between the warring camps.

19

THEY CALL THIS THE
LANGUAGE OF LOVE?

FTER SCHOOL, FOR THE FIRST MONDAY in almost two months, Lili had to go to French conversation class. Madame LeBrun was back from visiting her family in Normandy and had called the house the night before. Lili raced up the stairs of the Alliance Française, glancing up at the French flag that hung over the front door. Today the wind was strong and gusty, and the flag was whipping from side to side, slapping its post.

Lili shivered, hurrying into the cream-colored building. Half of her was desperate to see Max; the other half hoped he wouldn't be coming to French conversation anymore. It would be so much easier if she never saw him again. But on the other hand, it would be depressing if she never saw him again.

The smiling receptionist nodded to her, and Lili skipped up the wide, curving staircase that led to the second-floor library. Thin, pasty Madame LeBrun was already sitting in her usual armchair, looking dusty and anemic as usual, books and newspapers overflowing from her ragged canvas bag.

Lili's heart thumped like a rag doll hitting the ground when she saw Max sitting across from Madame's chair. Why did he have to look so cute? Why did his soft hair have to fall into his eyes in such an adorable fashion?

Then she remembered he'd never even called her after she'd tried to explain and that he was blowing kisses at Amy Winehouse wannabes these days, and suddenly Max didn't seem so cute. Fickle and superficial—that's what Max really was, Lili reminded herself. She didn't even smile at him. She just slipped into her chair and squeaked *"Bonjour, Madame!"* to the teacher.

To make up for lost time, today was a special two-hour class. Lili was dreading spending that long in the same room as Max; she was going to have to *look at him* and *talk to him*, when all she wanted to do was stick her nose in the air and ignore him. But luckily the first hour and a half was spent watching a DVD of a cool old black-and-white film called *Breathless* or *À bout de souffle*, as Madame insisted they call it.

Madame also insisted they pull their chairs close to the table, where she'd set up one of the Alliance Française's

PowerBooks, so they could see the screen clearly. Sitting this close to Max made Lili's skin prickle with excitement. *Stop it!* she told herself. *Just watch the film and forget all about him.*

It was hard, though, because the film was all about the romantic relationship between a boy and a girl. A handsome young guy races into Paris in a stolen car, looking for his American girlfriend. He shot a policeman who was chasing him, and he needs to hide out.

His girlfriend, Patricia, is supercute, in Lili's opinion; she has a chic pixie haircut and wears amazing clothes—capris and ballet flats, a gorgeous little striped dress. She's studying at the Sorbonne and trying to become a journalist. Then Mr. Handsome shows up and takes over her life, trying to persuade her to run away with him to Italy. She reads about what he's done in the newspaper and finally decides to betray him to the cops. Instead of arresting him, though, they shoot him, and he dies in the street.

After the film ended, Madame told them they had to discuss it in French. After a few minutes of them stumbling along saying banal things like, *"C'est très triste"* and *"C'est très tragique,"* the conversation got a lot more interesting.

"I can't believe Patricia betrayed Michel," Max complained in perfect French. "There was no reason for it at all."

"Are you kidding me?" Lili demanded, swiveling in her chair to stare at him.

"En français, s'il vous plaît!" thundered Madame.

Lili chose her words carefully. It was hard to figure out the right thing to say in another language, but she managed. "Of course she had to report him! The detective said he'd make a lot of trouble for her—maybe deport her. *She* wasn't a murderer or a thief. She couldn't let him drag her down."

"All she had to do was throw him out of her apartment!" Max folded his arms and stared back at Lili. "She didn't have to get him killed."

"She didn't *know* he was going to get killed."

"He'd killed a cop—do you think the police were going to be all friendly to him?"

"I'm just saying she did the right thing. He was a criminal, after all." In the heat of their argument, Lili had forgotten to translate her thoughts from English to French and realized she was speaking French without noticing it.

"But didn't she say she loved him?" Max asked, his eyes flashing. "Or was she just pretending all along?"

"She wasn't pretending," Lili told him. "They were just from two different worlds."

"And you think that people who come from different backgrounds can't relate. One of them will end up betraying the other person. That's what you're saying."

"I'm *not* saying that," Lili protested, though she was feeling kind of confused. What did she really think? Why was she feeling so flustered? She'd been so fluent until now.

"That's what it sounds like," Max said, speaking English, since Madame had fallen asleep in her chair. "You think that because a girl goes to some fancy school that she doesn't owe anything to the guy she's seeing. It's all about *her*."

"And *you* think that a guy can get a girl into the worst kind of trouble and she'll still be as loyal as a puppy dog. Did Michel ever realize that maybe Patricia didn't *want* to drive off to Italy? That going someplace like Italy wasn't really her thing?"

"Maybe she should have *told* him that instead of just stringing him along and pretending she was into going to Italy."

"Well, maybe she might like going to Italy, if the circumstances were different, and she had more time to plan it!"

"No, Patricia should have been more honest about how she didn't want to go to Italy." Max shot Lili a hurt glance.

"EN FRANÇAIS!" interjected Madame LeBrun, suddenly sitting up and realizing that her charges were not speaking the right language. In French she told them to discuss the end of the film.

"Patricia wants to stay with *her* friend in Montmartre, but Michel refuses!" Lili pointed out, staring triumphantly at Max. "They have to talk to *his* friends and go stay with some girl *he* knows, even though she's totally pretentious and isn't nice to Patricia at all!" Now that was an easy sentence to translate. Lili knew *prétentieux* and *n'est pas sympathique.*

"Obviously, Patricia's friends weren't to be trusted," Max said coolly, sitting back with his arms folded. "They would be all judgmental about Michel, probably, and persuade Patricia to call the police. Which she does anyway, because he's, like, too different."

"*She's* the one who's out of place in *his* world," Lili insisted. "She's the one who doesn't fit in. He doesn't even care."

"He *does* care!" Max looked affronted. "It's just that she never returns any of his calls, even though he's been trying to reach her for weeks!"

Huh? Lili's mind raced. He'd been trying to reach her? But she never got any messages on her new BlackBerry. Then she realized it was a new number—when her family switched services at the beginning of January she'd gotten a new one, but of course he wouldn't know that. And if he called at home . . . if he called at home . . . if he called her at home, her mom would just lie to him and tell him she was giving Lili the messages, when of course nothing could be further from the truth.

Could Max really be talking about *their* relationship and not the one on the screen? "Maybe, if Michel understood that her mother was terribly strict and if he had her new cell phone number, they wouldn't have these problems."

"Her mother? Cell phone?" Madame LeBrun looked confused. "I have no idea what the two of you are talking about."

Lili gave Max her sweetest smile, and Max grinned back.

Madame might be in the dark, but Max and Lili understood each other perfectly.

20

THIS OLD HOUSE?

"COOPER! COME IN!"

Ashley answered the door herself, pushing the elderly butler out of the way in her excitement. "Oops, sorry!" she chirped, leading Cooper inside.

It was Friday night, and—for the first time ever—Cooper was coming to her house to pick her up. Sure, he'd been to her party, but he spent the whole time in the front yard on the Vespa or hanging out on the steps.

And when they went out on dates, they always met up somewhere else; Ashley wasn't sure why. Cooper always had a good reason, like he was in that particular neighborhood already and it would be easier if Ashley could just get dropped off. He'd be waiting for her on some street corner or outside a restaurant or at the entrance to the museum.

Ashley was looking forward to showing off the Spencer

palace, but when Cooper stepped into their grand marble entryway, his face wrinkled with disapproval.

Huh? Ashley followed his gaze. Everything was as beautiful and tasteful and expensive as it could be—the huge mirror, the fluted columns leading into the great room, the perfect crystal bowl on the console table holding an artful arrangement of twisted lilies. Her mother had flowers delivered every three days from In Water, one of the most chic and innovative floral designers in the city. Maybe he thought flowers were cliché?

"My parents are waiting for you in the great room," she told him, taking his arm and leading him down the airy hallway.

"What's so great about it?" he asked.

The slightly sarcastic tone threw her off a bit. "That's just what it's called." Ashley didn't know what to say.

"Why don't you just call it a living room like everyone else would?"

"But it's not our living room, really." Ashley didn't know what Cooper was getting at. "*This* is our living room, I guess—isn't it beautiful?"

She gestured at the expansive room with its pale walls and highly polished grand piano. Cooper just shrugged.

"Doesn't look like anyone hangs out there," he said, kind of dismissively.

"Well, no," Ashley admitted. She was puzzled: Why would they need to hang out there, when there were dozens of other rooms in the house?

"The kitchen's that way," she pointed. "If you want to stay here to eat, our personal chef could make us whatever we want. As long as it's organic, of course. She makes amazing gourmet meals."

"I'd rather go out," Cooper said quickly. Ashley hung her head. Of course Cooper wouldn't be impressed by a personal chef. He probably had a dozen of them at home.

"Well, here we are!" she said in a loud voice, so her parents would stop lolling around on the sofa and get up. But they must be getting deaf, because they both stayed exactly where they were until Ashley and Cooper were practically standing in front of them.

How annoying! Her mother was lying down, as usual, propped up with pillows, wrapped in an ivory pashmina and looking pale and languid. Her father was slouched on the floor, lovingly stroking Matilda's hand and resting his head on her baby bump. Oh no! He wasn't singing dreary old Cat Stevens songs to the baby again, was he? Just when Ashley wanted her family to make a good impression on Cooper! How humiliating!

"Hello, Cooper!" Her father clambered to his feet and did that hearty hand-shaking thing men did. "Welcome to our home. Please excuse my wife—Ashley probably told you she's expecting."

"Hello," breathed Matilda, holding out a limp hand. "So nice to see you again."

"Hey," said Cooper, who didn't seem to know where to look. *Not surprising*, thought Ashley. Who wanted to see old people acting so icky and lovey-dovey, not to mention openly discussing something like being pregnant? They had no shame.

"I was just giving Cooper a tour," Ashley told them. "He wants to see the house."

"No, I don't." Cooper sounded curt. Why was he being so dismissive about everything? Ashley loved this place. Her parents had made it so cozy and welcoming, even though it was big. Maybe Cooper was used to much grander places. Was their house *so* inferior to his? "I think we should get going. The movie's starting soon."

"Is this the one on Van Ness that you have free tickets for?" Ashley's father asked, and Cooper nodded, scuffing at the rug with one shoe.

"Our driver can take you," Matilda offered, pulling the pashmina tighter around her narrow shoulders.

"That's okay," Cooper told her. "It's just a short walk."

"But it's cold outside," Ashley complained. "And it's dark!"

"We'd feel better if our driver dropped you off," Ashley's dad told him, and Cooper shrugged, staring down at the floor. What was going on with him tonight?

Ashley was hurt. Her house might not compare to the Gettys' fifty-room mansion, but it was large and open and elegant. It was bigger than Lili's place, and the Li family had, like, five children! Okay, so Lauren's place might be a teensy bit larger, but it was so nouveau riche and tacky.

She was rightfully proud of her house, plus her parents were friendly, welcoming people who loved her and were hospitable to her friends. They were even acting nice to Cooper, even though he was so cold and aloof. Her mother was beaming up at him as though he was some long-lost son, and her father clapped a hand on Cooper's shoulder as they walked back toward the front door.

Suddenly Ashley felt a rush of nerves and self-doubt. Maybe Cooper not loving the house wasn't the problem. Maybe Cooper just didn't love Ashley. This whole "not in relationship mode" thing was getting her down. She wasn't even sure if she was his girlfriend. Could he be dating other girls? Could A.A. possibly have been right? Was Cooper scared, intimidated, or merely not that interested?

But as they were approaching her father's tan Range Rover, parked outside the front steps, Cooper did something sweet. It had rained a lot that afternoon, and there were dozens of puddles all over the gravel driveway. Ashley was just about to splash her way through a puddle when, all of a sudden, Cooper grabbed her around the waist and lifted her over it. Talk about gallant!

He flashed her the sweetest smile. "I don't want you to get your feet all wet," he muttered, dark hair falling into his eyes.

Ashley couldn't help herself: She fell in love with him all over again. So he wasn't tripping over himself to compliment her on her house. So what? It was just a house. Cooper's family probably had ten of them.

21

NOT QUITE READY FOR
HER CLOSE-UP

"AND . . . ACTION!"

A.A. walked along the sidewalk to the spot marked with an X of blue tape, trying not to (a) stare at the ground; (b) tug at the hem of her too-short skirt; (c) sweat under the glare of the bright lights angled over her; or (d) get distracted by the crowd of people watching.

This was a busy street, especially on a Saturday morning, and loads of onlookers were standing behind the barricades, trying to see what was going on. Add to that the fifty-plus people actually working on the movie, including four producers who all sat in a row staring at monitors, and it was hard not to get a serious case of stage fright.

She had no idea so many people or trucks or strange,

huge pieces of equipment were needed to make a little romantic comedy. It wasn't like this was *Transformers* or anything. She hadn't even heard of most of the actors—with one key exception. The leading man was the totally yummy Rake Parkins! Her crush! Even better, the main thing she had to do in this film was kiss him. Kiss Rake! Omigod! Since when did she get so lucky?

"And CUT! Good job, A.A. One more time, okay?"

A.A. wasn't sure what was so good about walking along the street looking like an idiot, but that was apparently another thing about making a movie—you had to do inane stuff over and over.

Marty liked to get a lot of angles, according to his bossy, clipboard-toting ADs Chelsea and Spike, so that meant A.A. had to walk up and down the street by herself over and over again for half an hour. She kept an eye out for the other Ashleys, all of whom had promised to be there—mainly to get a good look at Rake—but the public was far away, behind crowd-control barricades.

Meanwhile, she was getting more and more nervous. When they'd finished shooting her walk, Rake Parkins was going to emerge from his trailer all tanned, rested, and powdered, and they were going to film the next scene, where they had to stand outside a store and he was going to lean down and kiss her. Just like in *Beautiful Girls* where thirteen-year-old Natalie Portman charmed twenty-seven-year-old Timothy Hutton.

A.A. was playing the role of Veronica, the lead actress's little sister. In the upcoming scene, Veronica was supposed to be looking in a store window when her sister's boyfriend, Charlie—aka Rake—bumps into her.

He kisses her hello, but all his girlfriend sees is that he's kissing another girl. She gets outraged and dumps him, and the rest of the movie is about him trying to win her back.

Apparently they'd already filmed most of the rest of the movie, including three of the four scenes with the little sister. But the young actress playing the little sister had disappeared off to Eric Clapton's rehab facility in the Caribbean, where she and her entire family were being treated for their addiction to celebrity.

Because the girl couldn't shoot the rest of her scenes, Marty had to do some rapid-fire recasting. Which meant A.A. got to kiss Rake Parkins. There is a God.

One of the trailer doors swung open, and Rake emerged, a battered leather jacket slung around his broad shoulders. He looked even more gorgeous than the last time she'd seen him, during lunch in L.A. with Lauren. Except he was shorter. *Much* shorter than A.A. remembered. He was tiny.

She had to wear flats for this scene, and he was wearing what her mother rudely referred to as "pimp heels." A.A.

couldn't help but notice that he was plastered in a ton of makeup. She knew that movie actors had to wear makeup, but she had no idea it was *this* much.

Rake looked like he'd been lying in a toaster oven all day, then gotten slathered with butter, and finally dusted with cornmeal. It wasn't quite as exciting kissing someone who looked like walking breakfast cereal.

"Rake's on the set!" shrieked Chelsea into her megaphone, and A.A. froze, letting several other people in headsets bustle her into position outside the store. She wished Marty would give her some direction, or at least some words of encouragement, but he was busy talking to the line of producers. And she really wished all the gawkers would go away. Didn't they have anything better to do?

"Rake, we love you!" a girl's voice called from behind the crowd-control barrier.

Hang on—didn't that sound like Lili? A.A. scanned the crowd and spotted Lili's happy face. Lili had been on cloud nine ever since she and Max had gotten back together. And there was Ashley, standing right behind her, grinning like crazy. And Lauren! Lauren was giving the thumbs-up to A.A.—they all wanted her to do well.

A.A. waved happily, thrilled to see her friends, but Rake just gave a grimace-grin, as though he hated the fact that he was a sex symbol. When he followed the other AD onto the street, he pulled off his jacket and let it fall to the ground. A girl wearing a headset scampered to snatch it up and carry it back into his trailer.

A.A.'s mouth dropped open. Even though it was obviously that girl's job to pick up after Rake, the gesture seemed incredibly rude.

"This city," Rake was complaining as he and the AD approached. "It's freezing out here. We may as well be in Vancouver."

A.A. gulped. What should she say to Rake? *Hi, I'm A.A.— really pleased to meet you. I'm a big fan. Seen all your movies. Looking forward to working with you.* God! How lame.

Her stomach was churning, twisting itself into elaborate knots. At least she didn't have any lines to remember. All they had to do was mime saying hello to each other, and then Rake would bend in for a kiss. The idea was that the sister/girlfriend was across the street, too far away to hear anything.

"Here's your mark, Rake—whenever you're ready."

What? A.A. was kind of flustered. He wasn't even going to talk to her before the shot? He was standing about eight feet away, eyes closed, rocking back and forth on his high heels.

" He's getting in the zone," Chelsea whispered to her. "He's a real pro."

A.A. sighed. She guessed she was just an amateur, wanting

to have a conversation with someone before she had to kiss him in front of a huge crowd of people.

"Remember, A.A."—that was Marty, back in his chair, picking at something in his silver beard—"all you have to do is act surprised, look up at him, and let Rake do the rest. Good girl. Let's do it!"

A.A. stood as still as she could, willing her legs not to shake, pretending to look in the shop window, and waiting for the magic word—ACTION. And then suddenly Rake was by her side, twisting her around, flashing her a superwhite smile, and pressing his lips onto hers. Yuck! He tasted of bitter coffee and something sweet—maybe cherry lip gloss? Did guys wear that?

"And CUT!"

Rake pulled away, not making eye contact with A.A., clicking his fingers at one of the many crouched headset wearers. Two of the makeup artists descended on him, combing his eyebrows and powdering his chin.

A.A. wasn't sure what to do. It was very weird kissing someone who ignored you when the camera wasn't rolling. And it was even weirder to kiss someone with hundreds of people watching you. The Ashleys would want all the details later, and A.A. wasn't sure what to tell them. He tasted sweet and yucky? He smelled of cigarette smoke and too much Calvin Klein?

A.A. gazed into the crowd of fans and onlookers again, trying to remember where her friends were standing. Maybe the crowd had jostled and pushed them into another spot: Everyone wanted to get a glimpse of Rake. Oh, there they were. Ashley was taking photos with her cell phone, and Lili and Lauren were chatting with some guy. . . . A dark-haired guy in a Gregory Hall letterman's jacket . . . It was Tri. A.A. felt her skin get hot, and it wasn't due to the klieg lights. What was he doing here?

"Let's do that again," Marty called.

Suddenly A.A. felt ten times as nervous.

22

WELCOME TO THE DOLLHOUSE

INALLY LAUREN HAD FOUND A WAY TO spend time with Sadie that didn't involve buying Sadie clothes, listening to her brag about the S. Society's style influence at Miss Gamble's, or sitting around while she flicked through *Marie Claire,* whining that she should really have Nina Garcia's job as fashion director.

Instead, in a brief moment of clarity, Lauren had remembered how just a few weeks before, Sadie had tried to get her to do something they used to do all the time on Saturday afternoons in the old days, when Lauren still had frizzy hair, Sadie still wore thick glasses, and nobody named Ashley had even *noticed* them.

When Sadie had brought her doll to Lauren's house last semester, Lauren had turned up her nose at their old pastime. But perhaps she shouldn't have been so snotty. So on Saturday afternoon, after watching A.A. in action at the film shoot—kissing Rake Parkins not just once but eight times, because they had to do tons of takes—Lauren dragged herself over to Sadie's house with her arsenal.

"Look what I brought!" Lauren said as she unpacked shoeboxes of clothes and produced her dolls, Monterey Mandy and Sacramento Susie, from her duffel bag.

"Omigod! You still have yours, too!" Sadie immediately reached under her bed and dragged out Ventura Vicki, redheaded Pasadena Polly, and a scuffed-up baby doll, Big Sur Sally.

"You always had way more dolls clothes than I did," Lauren lamented. Her mother used to sew some of Monterey Mandy's outfits because they couldn't afford to buy them from the California Dolls catalog. Lauren always kept those at home, or hid them if Sadie came over to play.

"And I've been to the flagship store in San Diego," boasted Sadie, brushing Big Sur Sally's tangled mop of hair. "They have a theater and everything. And you can dress up as one of the dolls and get your picture taken."

"I would have loved that." Lauren sighed. She was telling the truth; she really would have loved to go. But back then her parents didn't have enough money to go to San Diego. Her father was a struggling grad student, and her mother took jobs here and there to help make ends meet. Neither of Lauren's dolls were new when she got them: Her mother had bought them both on eBay for a bargain price. At the time, Lauren pretended not to mind.

"You should try that poncho on Mandy." Sadie was the soul of generosity all of a sudden. "It'd look good with her dark hair."

Even though Sadie was often hard to take these days, she was almost her old self again this afternoon. Lauren couldn't help enjoying sitting around on Sadie's bedroom floor, rifling through the boxes of clothes and shoes. It was kind of fun being a kid again, dressing up dolls rather than worrying about their own outfits.

"Remember when you wrote the California Dolls company a letter asking them to make a doll with glasses?" Lauren reminded her.

"I was so sure they would do it!" Sadie gave a rueful smile. "All they did was send me a form letter and a coupon for five dollars off my next catalog order."

"And you used it to buy Ventura Vicki a boogie board!"

"Which I *lost* when I tried to get her to ride it at the beach. Her hair's never been the same since that day." Sadie was right: Vicki's hair looked like it had been plunged into a toilet bowl.

"And that one day, remember, we took one doll each to Great America, so they could ride the roller coaster?" Lauren started to laugh. It was her one and only trip to a theme park, ever. Sadie's mother had offered to take them for Sadie's birthday—maybe her tenth? Lauren had been so excited she'd thrown up her entire dinner the night before.

"Yeah! And one of Polly's shoes dropped off! That was so funny." Sadie was laughing as well. "Hey, you know—we could do that again. Take our dolls to Great America, I mean."

"Sure." Lauren shrugged. "Or maybe Disneyland. My father could fly us down sometime, maybe over the spring break."

"No, silly—I mean next week, for Congé. Oops!" Sadie clapped one hand over her mouth. "I wasn't supposed to tell you."

"That's your idea for Congé?" Lauren tried to sound casual, but her heart was already on the roller coaster, soaring up and down. Sadie had finally blabbed!

"You won't say anything to the Ashleys, right?" Sadie put down the doll hairbrush, and Lauren solemnly shook her head. "We're presenting to Miss Charm next week. So don't say a word! I mean it, Sheridan would kill me!"

"You know you can trust me," Lauren said.

Sadie looked around, even though they were the only two people in the room. "Okay, so here's our plan. Our dads are going to rent Great America for the whole day, so Miss Gamble's has the run of the place. How cool is that?"

"Way cool," said Lauren, her fingers fumbling with the Velcro fastener on the back of Susie's tennis dress. Her mind was whirling. "How did you know which day to book?"

"We know Congé is the week before Spring Break, so it's one of only five days. So they've put a deposit down for each day. As soon as the plan's accepted, and we find out the exact day, they'll pay the full fee. You won't believe how much it's going to cost!"

"Tons, I'm sure." Lauren wanted to start packing up her dolls that second, but it would have looked too suspicious. She needed to get out of here and *think*. A private day at Great America? Man, that was going to be hard to beat. And they only had a day left—the committee leaders had to meet with Miss Charm on Monday morning.

But whatever the Ashleys came up with, one thing was certain. They had to give Lauren kudos for cracking the S. Society and uncovering their plans—even if she'd done it by accident!

The main thing was, she'd been given a mission, and she'd aced it. The Ashleys were going to be thrilled and relieved and—most of all—*grateful*. For once, things were finally going Lauren's way.

Of course, telling the Ashleys meant betraying Sadie's trust. Lauren felt a stab of remorse at that. She'd totally lied to Sadie without a backward glance. But hadn't Sadie betrayed Sheridan by blabbing?

And all was fair in war and Congé, right?

23

INTO THIN AIR?

L ILI WAS MAKING A LOT OF SACRIFICES.

First of all, she had cleared four hours in her usual Saturday afternoon schedule. She had begged her mother for permission to go on a short hike in the hills around Golden Gate Park, telling her she was going with a friend (only a small white lie, since Max was a boy*friend*), and promised to register with the park ranger and text her precise coordinates (latitude and longitude) every thirty minutes.

She had dressed in all the unflattering, nonfashionable outdoor gear she'd bought to go on the fateful camping-trip-from-hell back in December. She was pretending not to mind that the wind was blowing a gale, or that the track was still muddy from last night's rain. And she was not pointing out that her idea of a "short hike" did not involve scaling what appeared to be a Himalayan-size slope.

But Max didn't seem to appreciate any of that.

After French class the other day, they had kissed and made up. Apparently the Amy Winehouse look-alike was his cousin—Lili had been jealous for no reason. Max had suggested they spend the day together hiking, and Lili had agreed in order to show him that she could have fun in the outdoors after all, if it was only the two of them and she didn't have to deal with the doomsday chorus of Cassandra and Jezebel.

But things weren't working out that way.

"I can tell you're not enjoying yourself," Max said as they trudged up the hill, wind gusting Lili's hair into her face. "We can just go back if you like."

"No!" she protested. "Everything's fine."

"Then why haven't you said anything for the last ten minutes?" He hurried on ahead.

"Maybe because I'm out of breath climbing Mount Everest!" Lili couldn't help herself.

"This isn't steep at all." Max spun around to face her and stopped dead. "This isn't as steep as the hill you walk up from Starbucks every day to get to school!"

"But *that* hill isn't all muddy and rutted," Lili complained. She kicked one hideous boot against the ridges of the track. The boots had been black when she left home—now they were a crusted clay brown. Flecks of mud had sprayed all over her fleece vest. Gross.

"See—this is the problem." Max looked exasperated. "You're way too high maintenance!"

"I am *not* high maintenance," argued Lili. She tugged at the strands of her hair that were sticking to her mouth and felt the grit of windblown dirt salting her lip gloss. *Disgusting*.

"Just admit it." Max folded his arms, staring her in the eyes. "That's why things didn't work out between us before, right? It wasn't about my friends or your friends. We're just too different."

"I thought it was because one of those mean girls you hang around with told you a whole lot of lies about me," Lili snapped.

After they'd finally stopped kissing that day at French, Max had confirmed what Lili had suspected all along. He'd confessed that Jezebel had told him that she'd seen Lili out with another guy on the same night that Lili was at home, totally grounded. Why, why, *why* Jezebel had made up such a malicious story, Lili wasn't sure. She was probably in love with Max herself. Hello! He was *much* cuter than *her* boyfriend.

"It wasn't just that," Max said now, looking kind of sheepish when Jezebel's Big Lie came up in conversation. "We're very different as people."

"No, we're not!" She felt like she was going to cry.

"Look, Lil, you can't even get dirt on your shoes. . . ."

"I can so!" Lili held up one foot, almost tumbling over onto her butt.

"You hate this."

"I do not!"

Max was laughing, shaking his head. He walked up a steep incline, using his hands to pull himself up to a narrow ledge jutting out of the mountain. "Come on up here! The view is amazing!"

Lili looked at her nails. They were freshly painted. If she scrambled up after him, she would ruin them. "I can't!"

"C'mon!" Max called. "Of course you can!"

"But I'll get . . ." Lili was about to say *dirty*, but she knew that Max would just mock her. "I mean, what if I fall?"

"You won't fall. I'll pull you up once you get close," he assured her, gazing down at her, his dark eyes sparkling. "Don't be scared."

But Lili didn't make a move.

"You can't do it, can you?" Max sighed. "Just admit it. You're one of the most high-maintenance girls in the Bay Area." He climbed down from the ledge and stood next to her.

Lili dropped her head so Max couldn't see her crying. He was right. She knew it. She was high maintenance. She liked everything to be clean and tidy and perfect, which was why she and Nature had never gotten along, exactly. Nature was so random and messy.

And Max was a free spirit. He didn't care about things like wearing a smart blazer or using the right knives and forks at a formal dinner.

"It's all right," he said kindly, stroking Lili's arm. She tried not to flinch at the thought of his muddy hands messing up her fleece vest. "Let's just cut our losses and go back."

She nodded and turned to follow Max back down the hill. Maybe he was right: It was time to cut their losses.

Maybe they just weren't meant to be.

24

ALL IN THE STEPFAMILY

ND NOW A TOAST!" JEANINE, A.A.'S MOTHER, held her goblet of sangria aloft and beamed around the table. This was the closest thing to a family dinner A.A. had experienced in a long time—even if it was after ten o'clock on Saturday night, and they were sitting in the chic, minimalist restaurant Limon in the Mission rather than around their own dining room table, eating Peruvian delicacies rather than chicken potpie.

"A toast," echoed Marty, raising his glass. A.A. tried to ignore the calamari bits stuck in his beard.

"To our little actress, A.A., who just made her film debut!" Jeanine was talking in too loud a voice, but the restaurant was still pretty crowded, luckily. "And to my family," she added, gesturing at Ned and A.A., "meeting *your* family."

Marty clinked her glass with his and smiled across the table at his son, Jake. A.A. smiled at Jake too—why not? He was fifteen, with straight, shoulder-length dark hair and intense dark eyes. His mother, Jeanine had stage-whispered earlier that evening, was an Argentinian actress. She and Marty had divorced five years ago, and Jake spent most of his time in Los Angeles these days, living with Marty in the Hollywood Hills.

And he wasn't just cute: Jake was really friendly and fun. He and Ned were already buddies, apparently, because they'd met at some statewide track meet earlier in the semester. When the talk turned to soccer, A.A. liked the fact that Jake didn't patronize her, the way some guys did, because she was a girl. He didn't even turn on her during a big conversation they had had about South American soccer, when she'd argued that the Brazilian soccer giant Pelé was a much greater player than the old Argentinian star Maradona.

While the kids talked, Jeanine and Marty leaned all over each other, feeding each other morsels from their dinner plates and giggling like children. So embarrassing.

A.A. and Ned and Jake just ignored them. It was nice to see her mother happy like this, even though A.A. wasn't sure this romance would last any longer than Jeanine's other passions and obsessions. Oh well, at least if she married Marty, A.A. would get another cool stepbrother.

When Jake and Ned started talking about people they knew through track meets, A.A.'s attention wandered. Holding her phone under the table, she surreptitiously sent Tri a text. No reply. The only text in her in-box was from Lauren: SS PLAN GT AM FOR CONGE. That was good news and bad: It was great that Lauren knew what the S. Society had up their polyester sleeves, but Great America was going to be a hard destination to beat. How were the Ashleys supposed to top that?

She sent another message to Tri and then folded up her phone so she could eat dessert. Ten minutes later she checked again—still no reply. That was weird. The other day, when Tri was over at their apartment playing video games with Ned, A.A. overheard him saying he was lying low this weekend, hanging out at home. Maybe he was blowing her off—but why? What had she done *this* time?

Actually, he'd been kind of keeping his distance from her for ages. Ever since that day she'd gone over to his place and helped his mom with some cooking, he'd acted like he barely knew her. This didn't make sense at all. At Ashley's party, they had agreed that it was probably best that they forget about everything that had happened before and just go back to being friends. It was nice to have their old friendship back.

But now he was acting cold and distant, as though he needed to send her some "message." Well—message received, idiot! He didn't even want to be friends anymore, obviously.

But wait a second. Hadn't that been Tri in the crowd earlier today, when she was filming? If he wanted to avoid her, why come along to that? Ned must have blabbed about it. How annoying. If only her brother was sitting closer to her, A.A. would have kicked him under the table. Luckily for him, he was just out of leg's reach. And she certainly didn't want cute Jake to think she was trying to play footsie with *him*. . . .

"A.A.!" Her mother was snapping her fingers in A.A.'s face. "Wake up! We're leaving. Jeez, Marty—I hope she wasn't this out of it on the set!"

"She was just fine," rumbled Marty, his squinty eyes disappearing as he smiled. A.A. felt her face flush. Maybe Tri had come along earlier to see how horrible she was at acting. Give her a break: She was hardly a professional! All they told her to do was walk up and down the street over and over, and then kiss Rake over and over. At first it was kind of exciting, and then she noticed Rake had bad breath, and then it was just tedious.

And so what if Tri saw her kissing Rake. He didn't even *like* her these days. Right?

"I heard you sucked," Ned teased, almost tipping his chair over when he got up.

"Who told you that?" A.A.'s heart thudded. She squeaked

along the banquette, trying to shrug on her jacket and getting the arms all twisted in the process.

"It was on *Entertainment Tonight*," he drawled. "Preteen nonactress ruins multimillion-dollar production with terrible acting."

"Shut up!" A.A. glared at her brother. This wasn't the time for his stupid jokes!

"I thought you were great." Jake flashed her a sympathetic grin.

"You were there?" A.A. was confused. She didn't remember seeing Jake on the set.

"Yeah—I was standing with Ned near the catering truck."

A.A. shook her head. So Ned was there today, *and* Jake, *and* Tri. Did they *want* her to feel self-conscious?

"I was going to get Tri onto the set," Ned told her as they all walked toward the restaurant's front door. "But something was up with him. He said he just wanted to stand on the street. Weird."

Weird was the word for it. A.A. sighed, bracing for the brisk evening breeze blowing in from the street. Her mother zoomed from one grand passion to the next, but to A.A., all this boy stuff was way too confusing.

Who knew why they did the strange things they did? Who knew *what* they were thinking?

25

ASHLEY SPIES ANOTHER
FISH IN THE SEA

ASHLEY WAS COLD AND TIRED AND LONELY. After meeting Lili for cheer-up after-dinner fro-yos at Pinkberry, she was waiting for Cooper to meet her so they could make the late movie, but he hadn't shown yet. She kept checking the time on her cell phone every few minutes. He was five minutes late, then eight, then ten, then twelve. . . . What was going on? Maybe something terrible had happened to him. Maybe he'd been run over on the way here, or maybe his convoy had been attacked by some Greek terrorist organization.

BEEP.

At last! A text from Cooper. Ashley eagerly clicked it.

SORRY CANT MAKE IT RLLY SORRY.

Whaaaaat?? He was standing her up? It wouldn't be so

bad, but this wasn't the first time Cooper had backed out of a date at the last minute. It was *soooo* depressing how he always had other things to do. Ashley realized he must have a packed calendar, since his family was always traveling. But she wished that once in a while he would invite her to some swish event and not leave her stranded on a street corner somewhere. Did he like her or not?

So now she had to slink home and waste what was left of the evening watching some makeover marathon on TV or—even worse—listening to her parents discuss baby names while her father rehearsed dreary lullabies on his acoustic guitar. She called them to ask for a ride home, and they told her to wait in the lounge of a busy restaurant they liked, where the maître d' knew the whole family by sight.

Inside the lounge it was too crowded, not to mention boring. There were no magazines, and everyone waiting at other tables kept looking at her strangely, as though she were a teenage runaway. Ashley tried to focus her mind on the text that had come in from Lauren earlier in the evening. So the S. Society was planning a jaunt to Great America? Whatever! The Ashleys could come up with something *much* better than that.

But right now, Ashley couldn't think of anything amazing. In fact, all the ideas they'd been discussing over the past couple of weeks were pretty lame. The only idea that Ashley really liked was a day trip to Stinson Beach, mainly because Cooper had told her that *Flown the Coop* was going to be moored there next week. Any chance to see Cooper was better than nothing. This argument, however, was unlikely to win over a committee of teachers. They'd think that Great America sounded like a whole lot more fun for everyone else—and Ashley had to admit they'd be right.

When her father finally texted with an ETA of five minutes, Ashley wrapped her thick cashmere scarf tightly around her neck, buttoned up her new fur-trimmed Miu Miu coat, and braved the chilly weather outside. If only her parents would let her catch a cab by herself! She could have been home by now.

"Ashley! What are you doing here?" Bounding out of the same restaurant with her usual giant strides was A.A., followed by her stepbrother Ned, and some other guy. Some cute guy. Some *very* cute guy. Well, hello.

"Waiting to get a ride home," Ashley told her.

"Where's Cooper?" A.A. scanned the sidewalk. "Aren't you having dinner with him tonight?"

"He had to leave. Family emergency." There was no way Ashley was confessing to A.A.—or anyone—that Cooper was a no-show this evening. She didn't want their pity. And, most of all, she didn't want the story getting out. Her ranking as Queen Bee at Miss Gamble's was hanging by a thread again, and she couldn't risk any reputation-destroying gossip getting out. She nudged A.A. "Aren't you going to introduce us?"

"Oh, yeah—this is Jake Law. Jake, this is Ashley Spencer."

"Her best friend," interjected Ashley, shoving one gloved hand at Jake. He shook it, then smiled at her. Those dreamy green eyes! That gorgeous curly hair! Ashley had no idea that Ned had such good-looking friends.

"Are you at Gregory Hall with Ned?" she asked him, wrinkling her forehead. She would have remembered *this* guy, she was sure.

"No, I'm just visiting from L.A.," Jake explained. "My dad is here making a movie. Here he is!"

Jeanine and Marty stepped out of the restaurant, Jeanine staggering and laughing uproariously. They were holding hands, and Marty was pecking little kisses all over her dark hair. Not another lovey-dovey old couple? Why did elderly people have to behave so badly in public? Didn't they know that PDA was disgusting over the age of twenty-one?

"He's my future stepbrother," A.A. whispered in her ear. "Possibly. Who knows?"

"You should have come by the set today," said Jake, turning back to face Ashley. "I could have shown you around. But we've finished filming here now. All the interiors in the movie will be shot in Vancouver."

"I *was* there. Well, I was in the crowd, watching A.A."

Ashley pushed her hair back from her face. She was so busy staring her eyes out at Rake Parkins, she hadn't realized there would be even cuter boys hanging out on the set.

"Another time." Jake smiled. Ashley was so distracted, she didn't even notice her father's SUV pulling up until A.A. brought it to her attention. After shaking hands with Jake again, kissing A.A., and forgetting to say good-bye to Ned and the doddering lovebirds still making fools of themselves, Ashley climbed into the front seat next to her father. The car smelled odd.

"I've been helping your mom with her painting, since the smell is getting to her even though we bought the safe, non-toxic paint," her dad told her with a sheepish grin. Ashley looked at him: His sweatshirt and jeans were speckled with paint of every possible color. "We're almost finished with a woodland mural in the baby's room. If you're not too tired, you could help when we get home!"

"I'm exhausted," Ashley said. It was true: Part of her was depressed about Cooper not showing for their date, and part of her was kind of happy she'd gotten the chance to meet Jake. It was all too tiring and confusing. A.A. was lucky—her life was much more straightforward. She got to live in a cute apartment and do whatever she wanted, and now some hot guy from L.A. was going to be living there as well.

Ashley's life was a mess. She had a boyfriend who was

AWOL, parents who'd lost their minds, and a tiny room in the attic. Before too long, all she'd be able to hear would be the baby crying and screaming, and everyone stampeding around the house attending to its every demand.

Once the new baby came, she'd have to get used to being numero dos. Maybe she was already numero dos with Cooper. He was probably out tonight with some European princess or something. Ashley was beginning to realize something. No matter how much you wanted something—or someone—you couldn't always get what you wanted in life. Not even if you were Ashley Spencer.

26

LAUREN TUNES IN TOKYO

T SHOULD HAVE BEEN A PERFECT SATURDAY
night date, Lauren thought. Just her and Christian,
goofing around in a bowling alley and then sharing a
giant ice-cream sundae in Joe's Diner. No stress, no
Ashleys, no Sadie, no school. She spooned a heaping,
melting mound of delicious vanilla ice cream—dripping
with hot fudge sauce—into her mouth, and had a brief
moment of utter happiness. How nice it was to be out with
a cool guy like Christian. She didn't have to put on an act
with him.

But it wasn't a perfect Saturday night date. In between giant
mouthfuls, Christian was talking away about stuff he wanted
them to do next weekend, but Lauren really couldn't pay attention. All she could think about were ideas for the perfect
Congé celebration. It wasn't enough to know what the S.
Society was planning. The Ashleys—and she included herself

here—needed to come up with a brilliant alternative plan and totally kick the S. Society's behinds. Lauren couldn't kill the queen just to have another tyrant on the throne. The S. Society had to be put in its place.

But booking Great America for the day was pretty impressive, she had to admit. How could she top that?

". . . and I was thinking about that day . . ." Christian was still talking, even though his mouth was full of ice cream. Lauren shook herself; she had to pay attention. ". . . you know—when we went to the Japanese Tea Garden?"

"Oh yeah, that was great," she said, hoping he hadn't noticed she was in Faraway Land. It *had* been fun to wander around the Japanese Tea Garden. Ashley had been to Japan itself, but Lauren hadn't traveled much yet; her parents had only been rich for about nine months. Japan was so romantic and exotic.

She'd had so much fun that day dressing up dolls with Sadie. How cool would it be to dress up themselves—to be a geisha for a day? To learn how to put on all that makeup and those elaborate wigs and beautiful silk kimonos, to take part in a tea ceremony, to learn how to dance with fans . . . how much fun would that be?

"That's it!" Lauren shrieked. Her spoon clattered onto the table. "Christian, you're a genius."

"I know," he said with a grin, leaning back in his chair

and then pretending to frown. "I was wondering when you were going to notice."

"You're brilliant!" She clapped her hands together.

"You're right and all, but . . ." Christian frowned. "Is it because I remembered the day we went to the Japanese Tea Garden? It wasn't that long ago, you know."

"No, no. It's because you've given me the perfect idea for Congé!" Lauren was practically squealing with excitement. She was going to save the day! The S. Society would be beaten! The Ashleys would be forever in her debt!

"Conj . . . what?" Christian shook his head. "Oh, you don't mean that day trip thing you're always obsessing about?"

"It's much more than a *day trip*, " Lauren told him. She reached for her phone and speed-dialed Ashley. Congé was coming up very soon; eleventh-hour brilliant ideas like this couldn't wait. "Hello?"

"You're going to go to the Japanese Tea Garden?" Christian looked bemused. He also looked kind of irritated that she was making calls to her friends when she was out with *him*. Oh well. He didn't realize the vital importance of this!

She blabbed everything to Ashley in a huge rush.

"And my father could fly everyone in, no problem. He goes to Japan for business every two weeks, and he knows a ton of people. He could fly in a whole lot of real-life geishas and really expensive silk kimonos for everyone, and all the makeup, and everything.

"It'd be like playing dress-up, but in a really amazing way. We could have sushi chefs there to prepare all the food, and maybe even have a dance competition in the afternoon, once everyone was all dressed up and had time to rehearse. The winning girl could get a free trip to Kyoto to see the cherry blossoms! And we could film it all and broadcast it on YourTV! What do you think?"

"Not bad at all." Ashley sounded impressed! She really did! "I think we may have a winner here. It's much more original than going to Great America for the day."

"You think?" Lauren felt wave after wave of happiness ripple through her—though maybe it was just the effects of too much ice cream.

"Of course!" Ashley scoffed. "Everyone's already been to Great America. Roller coasters—big deal. This is much more sophisticated. I want to have first pick of the kimonos."

"Of course," Lauren assured her. "And I'm sure the teachers will like it too, because we'll all be *learning* something."

"Whatever!" Ashley always said that learning was for people who couldn't afford to pay full tuition at the colleges of their choice. "I'll call the others and let them know the good news, okay? You get started on booking everyone."

Lauren turned off her phone and beamed at Christian. Everything was all wrapped up in a perfect silk-bowed parcel. She'd come up with a killer idea and now she was back in Ashley's good graces at last.

"Thank goodness." She sighed. "Ashley is so into the idea."

"Can we talk about something else now?" Christian asked, swallowing the last bite of ice cream.

"Okay. But you know, I'm just so glad that Ashley thinks—"

"Who cares what Ashley thinks?" Christian demanded. The tone of his voice startled Lauren—he sounded really fed up. "We were talking about stuff you and I want to do. Together. Or at least, *I* was talking about that. Maybe you were just thinking about Ashley and A.A. and Allie—"

"Lili!"

"Whatever her name is. It sounds like you care more about what they think than anything I have to say."

"That's not true!" she protested.

"Really? I don't know if I believe that." Christian looked really mad. He scratched at his dark blond hair. "Maybe you shouldn't be spending so much time with a guy who doesn't understand all the nuances of life at Miss Gamble's."

He was just mocking her now. Lauren bristled.

"I can't believe you're being so awful."

"I can't believe *you're* being so awful," he retorted. "Let's just go, okay?"

"Okay!" Lauren started pulling on her coat, trying to choke back tears. They'd been having such a good time, and suddenly they were arguing. And the timing couldn't possibly be worse: Christian's mother had invited her to their house for a big family lunch tomorrow, something she'd been looking forward to for ages. Why couldn't he be more reasonable? Tonight she'd finally managed to get back IN with her girls—and now she was OUT with her boy.

This was so unfair. Couldn't a girl have both?

27

LILI DOESN'T LIKE BEING
SECOND BANANA

W HAT ABOUT LAUREN?" ASKED A.A.,
flopping onto Lili's vast carved Chinese
bed—and obliviously pushing a half dozen
of Lili's carefully arranged silk cushions onto the floor.

"What about Lauren?" Lili shrugged dismissively. Now
that Lauren the Spy had discovered what the S. Society was up
to, she was back in Ashley's good books—and Lili couldn't
help feeling a bit insecure.

Lauren was the one who found out about Great America;
Lauren was the one who had the exciting alternative plan. Lili
had always come up with the ideas for Congé before. Okay,
so maybe she'd been a bit busy with Max, but given enough
time, she would have come up with something great, as usual.
She didn't like Lauren stealing all her thunder.

A.A. exchanged looks with Ashley, who had comman-
deered Lili's Aeron chair and was playing with the controls,
whizzing up and down. "Sunday lunch with her what's-his-
name. Crispin. Christopher. Chip . . ."

"Christian. His name is Christian. You know, we could
have had the meeting later."

"No, we couldn't." Lili bustled around the room, handing out copies of Lauren's Japanese Tea Garden idea for
Congé. Lauren had e-mailed the plan to her this morning,
at Lili's request.

"How long is this?" Ashley sighed, paging through the
document that Lili had printed out in her father's home
office. "It's, like, *War and Peace!*"

"This was the only window I had available today," Lili told
A.A., trying hard not to snap. "I have to set up for a party at
Chinese school later this afternoon," she continued, "and
my ISEE tutor is here this evening." Acceptance into Miss
Gamble's high school was competitive and not guaranteed to
students in the elementary school. But Lili had her sights
even higher: She was determined to go to boarding school
back east.

"I'm *so* glad I don't have your life," groaned A.A., her
voice muffled by the cushion she was nuzzling. "All I have to
do tonight is make sure there aren't pizza crumbs all over the
white carpet before my mom gets back from L.A. We're not

supposed to eat colored food in the living room."

"Anyway," said Lili, shaking her stapled sheaf of notes, "we needed to meet right away, because there are some very serious matters to discuss. First, how do we deal with this Great America booking made by the S. Society?"

"No problemo," sang out Ashley. She twirled in her chair, feet (yellow Tory Burch Reva flats, charcoal Wolford hose) sticking straight out. "I have it all under control. My father's already called Great America. Well, he had his people call their people."

"On a Sunday?"

"They're open on weekends, duh! Apparently, *someone* had put down a deposit for every day for the five days Congé could possibly be, to close the park for a private group on forty-eight hours' notice."

"Damn!" A.A. looked forlorn. "What are we going to do?"

"*We* don't have to do anything. My father already has. He's paid the full fee up front."

"What—you mean for every one of those days? To totally close Great America to anyone but us?"

"Even better," Ashley said with a wicked smile. "The official reason for closing the park is so they can do emergency maintenance on some of the rides. If they don't do the maintenance, people might be killed, yada yada yada. They'll return the S. Society's deposit, and nobody will be any the wiser. The S. Society won't be able to go around pointing fingers at us and crying foul. They'll only find out tomorrow morning, just before we submit our Congé proposals. Whatever we submit, that'll be the only proposal. We win!"

"Hang on—why can't *we* just submit Great America as *our* idea, then?" Lili frowned, but Ashley shook her head.

"Apparently they said they'd either have to honor the original booking or close the park completely for the week. Something to do with ethics or . . . whatever!"

"How did you get your father to agree to pay so much money?" A.A.'s eyes were wide with wonder and admiration. "It must be costing him a fortune."

"I guilt-tripped him into it," Ashley announced, kicking her heels. "New baby, new room, I feel left out, you don't love me. I threw a major tantrum." She grinned. "And he went to school with half the board of Great America, so there was no way *they'd* refuse."

"Excellent work," Lili told her. She perched on the side of her giant bed, legs bare against the thick silk coverlet. Now was the time to put *her* plan into action. She felt a little nervous: Could she persuade A.A. and Ashley to see things—do things—her way? "So now we have to lock down our proposal for tomorrow."

"This idea of Lauren's looks pretty cool," said A.A., flapping the handout.

"As long as she does all the work," agreed Ashley. "We can just give her the go-ahead this afternoon."

Lili cleared her throat.

"This is great and all," she began, and then paused. "But Ashley—didn't you have an idea as well?"

Ashley nodded. "Stinson Beach."

A.A. made a face. "It's not exactly Malibu."

"That's true," Lili said slowly. Stinson Beach was windy most of the time, and the beach was covered with rocks. Even though the weather in early spring was a bit warmer, it was still cold out there. The only big plus was that it was close to the city, and all that meant was that everyone could go there whenever they wanted. It wasn't a very glamorous, exotic, or exciting location—and not half as fun as a day out at Great America. "But there are some good reasons why we should consider it."

"Like Cooper's yacht," said Ashley with a sigh. Whenever she mentioned his name these days, thought Lili, she seemed to go weak in the knees—and soft in the head. "It's moored there this week. So there's a good chance he'll be able to hang out with us. We could all go on the yacht and sail around. We'll sneak behind Miss Charm's back!"

"That's nice for you, but what about the rest of the girls? Not all of us are going to fit on Cooper's yacht," A.A. pointed out. "If he's the only reason we're going to the beach, it's kind of lame . . . sorry."

"True," agreed Lili. She adjusted her position on the bed so she could look straight at A.A. "But not everyone will feel left out. There are other reasons for hitting Stinson. For one, I know that the entire seventh and eighth grades from Gregory Hall are camping there this coming week for their geology field trip." That should make a lot of girls happy.

"Camping!" Ashley shivered with horror, but Lili's words had the effect she intended on A.A.

"Really?" she said, sounding a little *too* casual. "They'll be there all week?"

Lili nodded. "Tri, Christian, all the cute lax guys."

"That should keep you busy, A.A.," said Ashley, spinning in her chair again. "Tri, Christian, Cooper—all the men in our lives will be converging on this beach this week. Except for yours, Lili. They don't have field trips at Fame Junior High, do they? Unless it's to some grungy place in the Castro."

"Actually," said Lili, "Max's spring break starts Wednesday. So he could, in theory, come down to the beach as well." She certainly hoped he would. Things had been cool between them since the hiking drama.

"Now I see why you're so up on this idea." A.A. hit Lili with a pillow. "And fine—you've sold me on it. Much more fun than trying on robes in a tent in the Tea Garden."

"We can wear bikinis under our school uniforms that day!" Ashley was excited.

"Lauren won't mind, will she?" A.A. asked. "Not if she can hang out with Christian."

Lili stood up, dropping Lauren's proposal to the ground as though it was a piece of trash.

"That's the other thing I wanted to propose," she said. She stood with her hands on her hips, looking from A.A. to Ashley. "I don't think we should tell Lauren about the change in plans."

"Why not?" Ashley looked stumped. "She was the one who found out what the S. Society was planning. I know I've been a bit hard on her, but she totally came through. She's totally on our side."

"Is she?" Lili asked. "Then what was she doing at the Mother-Daughter Fashion Show, helping all those other girls get ready?" Lili meant she had seen Lauren with Guinevere, Daria, and Cass, not Sadie and Sheridan, but she didn't make it clear. She knew it would annoy A.A., who was still angry at the S. Society for sabotaging her shoes.

"She did *what*?" A.A. sat up.

"Maybe she was just being friendly." Ashley shrugged. "I mean, she and Sadie did used to be friends." Lili couldn't believe that Ashley was trying to defend Lauren.

"Friendly," Lili repeated. "Right. You know, Lauren was

the first girl to arrive that day—I know, because when Mom and I got there, Lauren and her mother were the only other people around, and then later they were talking to Sadie and her mother. They were probably planning it then."

Lili didn't mention that Lauren had walked into the backstage changing area after Lili: She wouldn't have had time to damage A.A.'s shoes. And the Pages greeting the Grahams had been perfunctory. But the others didn't need to know that. Lili knew what she was doing was wrong, but she couldn't help it. It bugged her that Lauren was taking her place in the group.

"No way!" A.A. was outraged. "Why would she do something like that? Do you think she's trying to double-cross us? Play both sides?"

"Maybe. Certainly looks like it," Lili said smoothly.

"You know," Ashley said, tugging off one shoe and examining the sole, "I think we're giving Lauren way too much credit. She's not smart enough to double-cross us."

"Exactly," A.A. cried. "Lili's found out the truth!"

Ashley screwed up her nose. "But I don't get it. Why would she ruin their Congé plans and do all this work on a huge, elaborate plan for us if she was really on their side?"

"Who knows what she's really planning?" asked Lili, folding her arms and looking stern. Since when was Ashley Spencer so tolerant and laid-back? Maybe Cooper was having a good effect on her. Unfortunately, Good Ashley was not the person Lili wanted sitting in her room today—it was Mean Ashley she was hoping to convince.

"I mean, did Sadie really tell Lauren about the S. Society's plans yesterday, or has Lauren known for ages? Maybe she's been planning this Japanese thing all along, so *she* can be the one who gets all the glory for Congé. Doesn't it strike any of you as odd that she suddenly, overnight, comes up with this brilliant plan?"

"Ash, I think Lili is right," said A.A. "We can't really trust Lauren yet. Let's just freeze her out on this. It'll do her some good to learn she can't stab us in the back."

"I guess." Ashley still looked doubtful. "But how do we keep it from her? We have to present our Congé plan to Miss Charm tomorrow."

"I'll tell her *I'm* presenting it," Lili said. "And I'll tell her that I'll be the one making all the bookings and plans for the Japanese Tea Garden, like I always do for Congé. She won't know a thing about the *real* plans until Congé is announced."

Ashley sighed. "It just seems . . . kind of mean," she said. A.A. and Lili both stared at her.

"Are you feeling okay, Ashley?" A.A. asked. "Have you got a fever or something?"

"All I'm saying is, if it wasn't for Lauren, we wouldn't know about the Great America plan at all."

"And all *I'm* saying," Lili told her, glad that at least A.A. was on her side, "is that we can't trust her entirely yet, and she needs to know that." Lili felt a twinge of guilt. But there wasn't enough room in the Ashley's for *two* brainiacs. If Lauren planned Congé, it wouldn't be long before Lauren was number one on Ashley's speed dial either. The girl had to be put in her place.

"Oh, she's going to *know!*" A.A. laughed, and Ashley shrugged. She wasn't going to put up a fight. Lili could see that.

Lili had won the day. They were going to Stinson Beach for Congé, and Lauren was in for one nasty surprise.

28

EVERYTHING'S JUST BEACHY

USUALLY ASHLEY COULDN'T WAIT UNTIL Thursday morning—because it was *almost* the last day of school that week, and she had a whole weekend ahead that didn't involve boring things like classes or ugly things like school uniforms. But this week, Thursday was the biggest day of the week—maybe of the semester.

At the headmistress's morning meeting, held in the Little Theater, with all the school assembled on bleachers and all the teachers sitting on the stage, Ashley arose from her seat and walked very slowly up to the podium. She wanted to make this moment last as long as possible. With every step she took, she could hear the whispers behind her growing louder and more excited. Why was Ashley Spencer walking up to the stage? Could this mean . . . could it possibly mean . . .

Yes!

"Surprise!" she shouted into the microphone. "Today is Congé!"

The entire school erupted into shrieks of delight. Girls leaped up in their seats, woo-hooing and hugging one another. No school! A day off! Total fun to be had by everyone!

Well, not quite *everyone*. Ashley stared in triumph at the forlorn members of the S. Society, who were the only girls in the school still in their seats. Now they knew the terrible truth—that the Ashleys had come up with the winning idea for Congé. That sealed their ownership of the bench, the table at the refectory, and Social Club. Ha!

"Where are we going? Where are we going?" The whole school was shrieking at her. The headmistress, lurking nearby, had to hold up a hand to silence them.

"You want to know where we're going?" Ashley asked coyly, and everyone roared back at her.

This was brilliant! "Okay, okay. In exactly fifteen minutes, stretch limo eco-buses will be pulling up outside the school to take us to . . . Stinson Beach!"

It was like someone had suddenly turned down the volume. Everyone still looked happy about getting the day off, but Stinson Beach clearly wasn't the most exciting destination in the world. Some people looked distinctly disappointed. Ashley heard someone—was it Sheridan Riley?—saying, "But it's just some dumb beach."

The thing was, Ashley kind of agreed with them. Stinson Beach *was* pretty lame, as beaches went. But what people didn't realize was that the beach was *crawling* with boys this week. And Cooper was almost certain to be there!

Ashley stepped down from the stage and wandered into the milling crowd. Most of the girls were too excited about getting the day off to complain about the actual destination. But she was delighted to see that the members of the S. Society looked *très* annoyed. Of course they were!

They were muttering together—arguing, even. They probably couldn't work out how a bus ride to Stinson Beach could possibly have beaten a private visit to Great America. At the sight of their miserable faces, Ashley could barely suppress malicious laughter.

She found A.A. and Lili in the crowd. "Are you guys wearing your bikinis?" she asked. "I'm wearing mine under my uniform."

"Um, yeah," Lili said, lowering her voice and glancing around the room. It was emptying out now as everyone made their way to the buses. "Did you see the look on Lauren's face?"

Yikes—Lauren. Ashley had been in denial about this all week. She'd agreed to go along with Lili's scheme, keeping Lauren in the dark about the real plan for Congé, even though she thought Lili was acting kind of crazy and paranoid. Now Ashley looked up at the bleachers and spotted

Lauren: She was still sitting there, her face pale and stunned. Poor thing! She was probably wondering why, after she had come up with an awesome idea, the Ashleys had decided to go with the much-less-original plan of Stinson Beach.

"She looks pretty mad," Ashley said.

"She'll get over it," Lili insisted. "Come on—we have to hurry! A.A.'s already out there."

Settling into her front-row seat in the bus, Ashley couldn't help thinking about Lauren. On Monday morning the committee leaders had presented their rival Congé plans to Miss Charm. Ashley had let Lili act as leader, mainly to keep up the ruse in front of Lauren. Lili said that Sadie Graham had gone into the library first and come out smiling from ear to ear. Obviously, she was sure the S. Society would win! But the Ashleys knew better, of course. Lili had told Miss Charm that the Ashleys had come up with the same idea of booking Great America, but they'd discovered—just that morning—that the whole place was closed for emergency maintenance for the next week and a half. Too bad! A fun, wholesome trip to Stinson Beach would have to do. And, faced with no choice at all, Miss Charm and the other teachers agreed.

Lauren had no idea that Congé was even happening today because Lili had convinced the Ashleys to keep her in the dark. She must have spent the whole night studying for an honors science test—a test the Ashleys knew wasn't going to happen. Poor Lauren! If Ashley had been the one doing hours of unnecessary work, she would be mad as well.

And if Ashley had been the one realizing that she was still an outsider who got excluded by her supposed best friends . . . well, that would never happen. And if it did? She would be *furious*.

But she couldn't allow pity for Lauren to ruin her day. At Stinson Beach, she and A.A. and Lili planned to parade around in bikinis in front of the entire seventh and eighth grades of Gregory Hall. Bikinis and boys. Hello! Everyone else might think Stinson was boring, but she was sure today was going to be tons of fun. In fact, it was going to be the best Congé ever.

29

ITSY-BITSY, TEENY-WEENY, YELLOW POLKA-DOT TANKINI

ILI HAD LIED TO ASHLEY THAT MORNING.

It wasn't a big lie. It wasn't an end-of-the-world-or-at-least-their-friendship lie. This morning, when Ashley asked Lili if she and A.A. were both wearing their bikinis under their school uniforms, Lili had said, "Um, yeah." Though what she really meant was, of course A.A.'s wearing *her* bikini.

Because Lili had other plans.

Ever since that horrible hike with Max, when he accused her of being super uptight and too high maintenance, Lili had been thinking. *Was* she too rigid? Too stuck in a rut? She'd taken a few tentative steps to mix up her game, buying some vintage clothes and breaking with the Ashley-mandated bag and shoes. But why not push herself a little further out of her comfort zone?

As soon as the fleet of eco-buses arrived at Stinson Beach, the Ashleys sprinted to the public restrooms to get changed. They weren't the only ones ripping off school uniforms: A lot of the other girls had brought a change of clothes with them to school every day that month in case Congé was announced.

But the Ashleys were the only ones who knew they were going to a beach, and they were the only ones who had matching red bikinis with ASHLEY monogrammed over the butt in white letters.

Annoyingly, Ashley had taken pity on Lauren and brought along an extra monogrammed bikini just for her. Lili couldn't believe how soft Ashley was getting. Why was she being so nice to Lauren all of a sudden? Where did *her* loyalties lie? Lili wondered.

Lili stood on a small towel in a toilet stall, tugging off her school skirt. Under her uniform she was wearing a swimsuit, but not one Ashley had picked out. It was something she'd seen in a magazine and gotten her mother's live-in seamstress to make for her.

The suit was less a bikini than a cute tank top and bikini bottom, like one Bridget Bardot had worn, according to *Vogue*. Although Bardot was a major sixties sex symbol, the suit was actually more modest than the skimpy little numbers A.A., Ashley, and Lauren were wearing. Nancy had liked the design and sourced the perfect vintage yellow and black patterned fabric from a family contact in Taiwan.

"Everyone ready?" Ashley shrieked from her cubicle. By "everyone," Lili knew she meant the Ashleys. This day was all about them, of course. Lili took a deep breath and swung open the door, stepping out over her now packed school bag. In addition to her vintage-style swimsuit, she was wearing raffia sandals from Twist Again and a floppy straw hat.

"Cute!" A.A., who was doing twirls in her red bikini, grinned when she spotted Lili. "You look so Bond movie! All we need now is for Daniel Craig to whisk you away somewhere glamorous like Marrakech or Istanbul."

All I need is for Max to see me, Lili thought, wishing—not for the first time—that he went to Gregory Hall rather than the School of Performing Monkeys, as Ashley had referred to it on the bus. His school was on break now, but she wasn't sure if he planned to come by the beach today—he hadn't said anything about it.

"Off message," sniffed Ashley, scrutinizing her from head to toe. "But not bad."

Lili wasn't sure whether to feel relieved or resentful. Why should she even care what Ashley thought? If it wasn't for Lili, they wouldn't even *be* at Stinson Beach today—they'd all be playing dress-up at the Japanese Tea Garden, just as Ashley's BFF Lauren wanted. Who was Ashley Spencer anyway these days? Not the boss of Lili, that was for sure.

Lauren was standing there as well, barefoot and in her red Ashleys bikini. She did *not* look happy, even though the bikini suited her svelte figure and perfect tan. Lili wanted to tell her to cheer up—things could be worse. At least they'd given her a bikini. Some of the other girls had to lumber around the beach all day wearing school uniforms.

And at least she had a boyfriend who went to Gregory Hall, a boyfriend who didn't accuse her of being uptight, conventional, and humorless.

Ashley was already pushing open the door to the restroom block, eager to get out on the beach and find the Gregory Hall camp. A.A., Lili, and Lauren followed her, hurrying into the sun . . . but what sun? The sun had disappeared. A cold wind whipped the beach, and rain clouds loomed. Brrrrr! Lili had to grab her hat before it blew away.

"Sweatshirts!" Ashley screeched, tugging matching monogrammed sweatshirts in the softest faded-red jersey out of her Pucci beach bag. She was like Mary Poppins today, Lili thought—she had so much stuff hidden in that bag.

They all pulled on their sweatshirts and looked at one another. Would today be a total washout? Lili consoled herself with the knowledge that if today totally blew, hopefully the whole school would forget about it over spring break.

"At least we can still play beach volleyball," A.A. pointed

out. She scanned the beach, shivering. Lauren just stood, clutching her sleeves and looking glum.

"And we can have campfires over by the grills," Lili told Ashley. "Look—there's a grill next to every picnic table. Did you bring marshmallows?"

All around them, the first and second graders were chattering excitedly about setting up the campfires.

"Of course!" said Ashley, not looking fazed one iota. "All we need is a bunch of sharp sticks. Maybe the S. Society can collect them? Or have the younger grades do it? We can't be expected to do *all* the work for Congé!"

Lili had to hand it to her: Ashley Spencer knew how to make the best of things. And today, in this one thing—this one thing only—Lili was prepared to follow her lead.

30

OH, WHAT A TANGLED
WEB WE WEAVE

LAUREN WAS IN A STATE OF SHOCK. SHE MIGHT BE swarming the beach with everyone else from Miss Gamble's, poking a toe in the water, gathering driftwood for fires, and pulling their picnic tables as close to the Gregory Hall geology field trip encampment as possible.

She might be dressed in the Ashley-approved-wear of red sweatshirt over her bikini, because it was turning into quite a cold day. But behind the goose-pimpled arms and frozen smile, she was in turmoil.

The Ashleys had lied to her. They had pretended to go along with her idea when they had no intention of doing any such thing. They had known about Congé for two days but said nothing.

Sure, Ashley Spencer had given her a monogrammed

bikini and muttered something about not meaning to leave Lauren out of things. But A.A. and Lili just stuck their noses in the air and didn't even attempt an apology.

Even worse than being lied to was . . . being a liar herself. The look on Sadie's face was making Lauren feel *really* bad. Sadie was hobbling around the beach in her booties, looking for pieces of wood, stopping every so often to tug at her argyle socks.

The S. Society wasn't at all prepared for today being Congé: They were still waiting to get the forty-eight-hour notice from Miss Charm. They were so sure they'd won. And, of course, they probably would have, if Lauren hadn't blabbed their plans to Ashley.

Lauren felt alienated from everyone. Alienated from Sadie, whom she'd betrayed. Alienated from the Ashleys, who'd betrayed *her*. She wandered away from the other girls. She'd spent the entire night before cramming for an earth science test that wasn't going to happen. She felt like a total fool. She thought she'd outsmarted everyone, but she was wrong.

Some of the Gregory Hall boys were still pretending to look for rocks, but most of them had wandered into the picnic area under the trees and were busy helping build fires in the grills or whittle sticks for marshmallows. Even the Gregory Hall teachers seemed more interested in lighting grills and chatting with the Miss Gamble's teachers than their own geology project.

Lauren stumbled over a rock, stubbing her toe. Ouch! Served her right. She rubbed at her stinging eyes with the back of one sleeve. She deserved to be miserable.

"Hey." She looked up, sniffing loudly, to find Christian pulling off his Gregory Hall fleece—blue and gold, the school colors—and handing it to her. "You look cold even with that sweatshirt. Put this around your shoulders."

"Thanks," she said gratefully. They stood together, looking out at the gray, roiling sea.

"Some day to come to the beach, huh?" he asked.

"It's a *horrible* day," she told him. "In every way."

"Well, not every way," he said. He turned to look at her with that mischievous grin she found so irresistible. "I'm here, and you're here. Right?"

"True." Lauren couldn't help smiling at him. "Thank goodness you're here," she said. Why had she wasted so much energy on some backstabbing girls who would never even accept her? Christian was her best friend. And she'd hardly made any time for him in the past couple of months.

"Your knight in shining fleece," he joked.

They both laughed. Lauren looked down at her feet, toes burrowing into the cold sand.

"Too bad it's cold," she said. "I'm wearing a really cute bikini under all these layers."

He leaned toward her, nudging her with one shoulder.

"I don't know, you look pretty cute in that sweatshirt."

"Thanks." Today wasn't looking so bleak after all. Lauren couldn't believe that just a few days ago she was arguing with Christian—practically breaking up with him, or at least driving him away—because of a bunch of selfish girls who didn't even consider her a friend.

Lauren almost reached for one of the rocks Christian was holding to bash herself in the head. For a smart girl, sometimes she could be so stupid.

31

WHAT'S NOT TO LIKE?

A.A. HAD ROUNDED UP A TEAM FOR BEACH volleyball, and a few of the Gregory Hall boys were helping her set up the posts and net, but it wasn't easy—the wind kept blowing everything over. Suddenly it felt a whole lot colder and windier, and then . . . was that a rumble of thunder?

The sky turned an angry shade of charcoal, and all of a sudden rain began to fall, pouring down and sweeping the exposed beach in dark sheets. Congé was a bust!

Everyone on the beach and in the picnic area scattered, racing for cover. A.A. decided to make for a rocky overhang under the cliffs, running as fast as she could across the wet sand, still clutching the volleyball net.

She hadn't had time to bundle it up, so it was trailing her like a mermaid's tail, entangling her feet. The rocks up ahead were almost invisible in the heavy rain, and she was completely soaked by the time she reached them. Only one or two more steps—aaargh! That stupid net! It was wrapping around her ankles, tripping her up!

"I got you!" A strong hand grabbed her, pulling her upright and dragging her beneath the overhang. "You okay?" Tri asked.

"Yeah, I'm fine—just wet." A.A.'s hair was plastered on her face, and it tasted as salty as the sea. Her sweatshirt and yoga pants were like a second, icy skin. On a day like this, they should have been in ski suits, not beachwear. A.A. shivered, pushing her hair out of her face, relishing the warm, scratchy feeling of a blazer being draped around her shoulders.

"It's kind of damp as well, sorry."

"That's . . . that's okay," she told him. Now that she could see clearly, A.A. tried to unwrap the volleyball net from around her legs. Tri crouched down to help. A few other kids were huddled nearby, close to the tide line, waiting for the rain to stop, but A.A. couldn't see the other Ashleys. All she could see were wet rocks, a pounding sea, and sheet after sheet of rain.

When Tri finished pulling the net away from her legs, he stood up and shot A.A. a long, serious look. Was he still mad at her? Was he going to disappear into the rain and leave her standing there?

"Come back here," he said, gesturing with his head.

"There's this kind of cave thing back there. We can sit in it until the rain stops."

He took her hand and pulled her along the narrow lane of dry sand. His hand felt dry and warm. It was the first time Tri had touched her since they'd kissed at that party so long ago, and A.A. could barely stand it.

The cave Tri was talking about wasn't so much a cave as a ledge about four feet off the ground, a tiny ridged nook worn into the cliff face. He jumped up into it and turned to pull A.A. in.

There was just enough room for the two of them to sit side by side, their legs dangling. The sounds of the falling rain and the relentless pulsing of the sea merged until it seemed to A.A. that they were surrounded by a rustling curtain of water. She shivered again, leaning into Tri.

He was still holding her hand.

"I'm glad that . . . you know," he said. A.A. didn't know. Was he glad it was raining? Glad she got wet? Glad that stupid net made her practically fall on her face? "That you're here today, and I'm here today. You know, at the same time."

"So am I," whispered A.A., though she couldn't look at him. He was sitting too close by. He was too handsome. He was still holding her hand!

"Because, you know. There's something I've been wanting to say to you."

A.A. held her breath. Finally Tri was going to tell her what she'd done wrong, why he was so annoyed with her.

"The thing is, ever since Ashley's birthday party, I've tried really, really hard not to like you," he said. Huh? A.A. felt totally crushed. Her whole body went limp, and her eyes filled with tears. Tri didn't like her. That's why he'd been acting so weird and cold—he didn't want anything to do with her anymore.

"And I've succeeded," he said grimly.

"You don't . . . like me?" She turned to look at him, her face red. This was worse than anything she'd imagined.

Tri shook his head. "Not one bit."

"Oh." A.A. felt hot tears form in her eyes and willed them not to fall.

But Tri took her hand gently in his. "You see . . . you see, the thing is . . ." He swallowed, then looked into her eyes. "I don't like you at all. I love you."

A.A. shook her head. Was she hearing things?

"And that's why . . . that's why I haven't been able to talk to you much lately," Tri was explaining. "I mean, it's pretty obvious you don't feel the same way. I told you what went down with me and Ashley. Either you don't believe me or . . . or I guess you hate the idea of going out with me. I thought we could just be friends like you said, but now I don't think that's possible. I'd always be wanting something more." He sighed.

Now the tears that fell down her cheeks were tears of joy.

"Why are you crying?" Tri asked.

A.A. shook her head. She was too happy to speak. Finally she said, "You're right. We can't be friends. We tried it and it doesn't work anymore." But she was smiling as she said it, smiling and grasping his hand so tightly.

"You mean . . ." Tri looked confused and hopeful at the same time. "You mean, um, that you don't *like* me, either?"

"I don't like you, and you don't like me!" A.A. shouted.

Tri grinned back, his smile practically splitting his face in two. He looked incredibly handsome, even with his hair wet and disheveled. Even in his Gregory Hall uniform.

"I love you, too," she whispered.

He pulled her closer to him. And once again, even better than the first time, they kissed.

32

LILI AND MAX REALIZE: YOU'RE THE ONE THAT I WANT

THE RAIN HAD FINALLY STOPPED, BUT LILI was still lurking around the parking lot, near all the parked buses. She'd taken off the stupid sweatshirt Ashley had handed her, trading it for a shimmery vintage jacket she'd bought at Twist Again.

Over her Brigitte Bardot bikini she'd pulled on a pair of sixties-style gingham capri pants that looked really funky with her raffia sandals—even though the rain had made her sandals feel all squelchy and heavy. It didn't matter: The main thing was that she didn't look like an Ashley clone anymore.

Today nobody really cared about this, she knew—not even Ashley, who was more preoccupied with rescuing Congé from its watery grave and dancing about on the sand, looking for Cooper's yacht. Right now she was marching around all the grills and ordering them relit. Lili wouldn't be missed, not for a while anyway. She'd wait for another ten minutes. Maybe twenty. Maybe half an hour. What else did she have to do?

She was waiting for Max.

If Lili was honest with herself, this whole new image wasn't all for Max. She liked expressing herself through clothes that Ashley hadn't dictated she buy. Lili felt independent, unpredictable, and more like herself.

Two days ago, when Miss Charm confirmed the specific date for Congé, she'd sent Max a text, telling him exactly when she was going to be on Stinson Beach. His school break had started, so he had no excuse.

Ten minutes passed. Twenty minutes passed. Lili leaned against the side of one of the eco-buses, willing Max to arrive. Maybe he couldn't find someone to drive him there. Maybe he had given up on her and never wanted to see her again. Maybe . . . was that his father's Jeep pulling into the parking lot?

She straightened up, tugging at her shiny jacket, hoping the rain hadn't made her hair look too limp. The rain had done a thorough job of washing away her makeup, though, which might be a good thing.

Waving at the car as it drove toward the bus, Lili wondered what Max would think of her new look. He'd seen glimpses of it before, like at French class, when he must have noticed her new bag and shoes. But he'd never seen her looking completely different. It wasn't possible when they went hiking—there were no vintage fleece vests or mountaineering boots! Women were smart in the old days, Lili decided. They knew that hiking was a boring waste of time.

The passenger door opened, and Max's fair head popped out. Lili couldn't wait to see him. Or see him see her . . . whatever!

"Hi!" she called. "Over here!"

"Hi," he said with a smile, stepping out from behind the car door.

He looked at Lili and his mouth dropped open. Which was funny, because Lili's mouth had dropped open too.

Max looked completely different. He'd cut his hair so it was all neat and tidy, short around his ears. He was dressed in a Ralph Lauren polo shirt, a tennis sweater, and pressed khakis. And what were those things on his feet, Adidas Sambas? He'd turned into a total preppie! Had he done this for *her*?

"What happened to you?" she asked, trying not to laugh. He looked cute, but kind of silly. Not like the Max she knew at all.

"I should ask you the same thing." He looked her up and down. "Don't get me wrong, you look cute and all, but . . ."

"But what?"

"It's just strange to see you looking so retro. Normally you're so together."

"Uptight and high maintenance you mean," Lili taunted him. He looked funny in that polo shirt. It just wasn't *him* at all.

"No! I like the way you normally dress." Max smiled. "You know, all *Vogue*'d out."

"Really?" Lili laughed.

"Yeah."

"But this is me too," Lili told him.

"Aw, you look cute in anything you wear," he said.

"But I like you all scruffy," Lili told him. It was true. If she wanted a Gregory Hall clone, there was a beach full of them to choose from. But she didn't want that kind of guy. She wanted Max.

And he seemed to want Lili—just the way she was too. Whether in designer or vintage. The clothes didn't matter at all. It was the person underneath that mattered—to both of them.

"I hope they take returns at Nordstrom," Max said, fingering his pale pink collar. "Or maybe I could give this to my dad for Father's Day."

Lili beamed at him. She was a little tired of wearing Vans. Not that she wanted to go back to wearing the Ashley-dictated Louboutins anytime soon. Maybe it was time to find a new shoe of her own. . . .

33

AN OFFICER AND A GENTLEMAN

HANK GOODNESS THE SUN WAS SHINING again. Ashley had urgent business to attend to—and no, that did not mean toasting marshmallows with a bunch of fawning sixth graders. She'd finally spotted Cooper's yacht approaching. As she waited impatiently for it to moor a little way offshore, she was texting him like crazy. At last he was rowing ashore to get her. About time.

Because the waves were buffeting the little dinghy, it took ages for Cooper to get anywhere near the beach. Ashley stripped down to her bikini and sweatshirt and waded in as far as she dared. Not that it mattered if she got wet—there would be a hundred fluffy towels on board, and she could warm up in the hot tub.

As he neared, drawing the oars back and forth with strong, broad strokes, Ashley caught sight of his outfit. He was all in white, with little black epaulettes on his shoulders. Was this some kind of costume?

"Over here!" she called. It was annoying the way you had to row backward—Cooper was heading straight into her. "Help me climb up!"

Cooper glanced over at her and shook his head.

"I'm coming ashore," he said, the boat bobbing up and down. He was wearing a uniform, she realized—white with brass buttons. And was that a *name tag*? "We need to talk."

"But why can't we talk on the yacht?" she pleaded. She'd been looking forward all day to lording it over the other girls, waving to them from the luxury yacht and letting only the other Ashleys come aboard. Maybe Lauren would start speaking to her again once they were all sitting on deck, drinking hot chocolate and soaking in the hot tub.

"Help me pull this in," he told her, and Ashley—for once—did as she was told. She helped Cooper drag the dinghy through the shallows, pulling it up onto the sand. Why was he dressed in this strange way?

Cooper leaned against the prow of the little boat, his white pants rolled up almost to his knees. He looked very unhappy.

"I don't get it," Ashley said. "Why can't I come to the yacht? Why are you wearing that?"

He folded his arms. "It's a uniform, Ashley. I should

have told you this before, I know, but the time never seemed right, and I thought you'd just run a million miles when you found out."

"Found out what?" Ashley didn't understand.

"That the yacht isn't mine. It doesn't belong to my family—my family can barely afford a car. It belongs to a Hollywood director who's hardly ever in town. Some guy named Marty Law. My uncle works on the boat, and sometimes I do as well. Today the director's in town, so I'm working. Hence the uniform."

Ashley was speechless. Utterly speechless. Cooper was *poor*?

"I really meant to tell you," he said, running a hand through his dark hair. "I tried to tell you . . . but I know how important money and nice things are to you. I knew you would just despise me if—"

"No!" Ashley interrupted him. She didn't despise Cooper. Of course she didn't—he was way too cute. So what if he was poor? She was rich enough for the two of them. "But what about that guy who was following us everywhere—I thought he was your bodyguard?"

Cooper shook his head. "That night I came to your house, he was parked in your driveway. Didn't you see him when we went out to the car? You're probably right that he was a bodyguard. Your parents must have hired him to trail us. They probably wanted to make sure you were all right.

You know, hanging out with a lowlife from the wrong side of the tracks."

"Don't say that!" she cried. "My parents really like you."

"Really?" Cooper looked kind of pleased.

"Yes." Ashley nodded. They must have known that Cooper wasn't a Greek shipping heir, but clearly it didn't bother them. She wasn't sure whether she should be pleased or annoyed that her parents had hired a secret bodyguard. On one hand, at least it showed they still cared and worried about her. On the other hand, they were kind of treating her like a little girl who needed to be looked after every minute of the day. Didn't they trust her? When were they going to let her grow up?

"They seem pretty cool," Cooper told her, and Ashley knew he was right. Her parents were overprotective, but it was just because they loved her.

"They are," she said. "They like you and so do I. What kind of girl do you think I am? I mean, seriously. You'd think I'd care that much about whether you owned a yacht or not?" She blew out her bangs and rolled her eyes.

"Really?" Cooper looked up at her. He was so dashing in that uniform!

"God, you're silly," she told him. "Do you want to come toast marshmallows?"

"I better get back." He grabbed her hand, pulling her

close, and swiped a quick kiss on her cheek. Swoon! "Now that the sun's coming out, everyone's going to be wanting drinks on the deck. I'll call you tonight, okay?"

Ashley stood, watching him row back to the yacht. She was kind of glad that Cooper wasn't a big-time heir. She didn't really want to move to Greece or waste a lot of time at charity balls. She'd rather go shopping in London or sunbathing in Cabo. If Cooper was poor, then he'd go anywhere she wanted. Beggars couldn't be choosers.

"Ashley!"

She swung around on her heels. It was only A.A., looking like thunder. Really, if A.A. wanted to play beach volleyball, then she had to get the teams organized and set the net up herself. Ashley couldn't do everything.

"We need to talk," A.A. barked, and Ashley sighed. First Cooper, now A.A. Today, it seemed, *everyone* wanted to talk to Ashley.

Being popular was so tiring. Thank goodness the weekend was coming up—at this rate, Ashley was going to need bed rest to recover from Congé.

34

DRAWING A LINE IN THE SAND

S O , " SAID **A.A**, STARING STRAIGHT AT Ashley. "I want to ask you something." A.A. had reached a breaking point with Ashley. She was ecstatic that she and Tri had finally been honest with each other about their feelings, but she also realized they could have been happy many months ago if not for a certain blond-haired queen bee with an ego the size of the yacht docked by the beach getting between them.

"Of course." Ashley nodded, but A.A. wasn't buying her reassurances. Ashley was as slippery as an eel when it came to truth and lies. Sometimes A.A. wondered if she actually knew the difference between the two.

"When you and Tri broke up, it was *before* the *Preteen Queen* party, wasn't it? He told you he wanted to go out with me, and you asked him to keep pretending to be your boyfriend until the party was over. That's true, isn't it?"

"Well . . . technically, I guess." Ashley looked guilty, shifting from one foot to the other.

"Technically?" A.A. was floored. "But *you* told me that you were dumping *him*. That he begged you to stay with him! When, in fact, the opposite was true. Wasn't it?"

"I suppose," Ashley admitted. "But everything's okay now, right? I just saw you and Tri all over each other a second ago. And I have Cooper. Can't we just forget it and move on?"

But A.A. was too angry to move anywhere.

"You," she snapped, "are *supposed* to be my best friend. But really, all you cared about was yourself. You didn't care if I was unhappy, or if I thought Tri was a total heel."

Ashley heaved a sigh, digging her heels into the sand. "Why are you making such a scene about this *now*? All that stuff's in the past."

"But I've been miserable for weeks!" protested A.A. Ashley just didn't get it. She didn't get anything that wasn't about Ashley Spencer. She was never going to change—A.A. had to accept that. Accept it, or end their friendship.

"So it's all about you," complained Ashley. "As usual."

Coming from Ashley, this was *too* outrageous. A.A. felt herself fill with righteous rage.

"I'm thinking about myself *right now*," she told Ashley, raising her voice to a shout. "And do you know what I'm thinking? I'm thinking that I can't be your friend anymore. That it's all over. All this Ashleys stuff! I'm out!"

"What?" Ashley looked at her as though she was insane. "You can't just drop out of the Ashleys. It's not possible."

"Watch me," warned A.A. Lili was hurrying toward them, and even Lauren—who'd been in a major sulk all day—was walking over. Both were wearing the red sweatshirts Ashley had brought. Lili had put away her shimmery jacket. What was it the S. Society said about them? The Ashleys were all exactly the same—all matchy-matchy. Well, A.A. was tired of everyone thinking she was the same as Ashley. She would *never* be as selfish as that. Never!

"What's going on?" Lauren frowned.

"We could hear you guys shouting from over there," Lili told them. "What's up?"

"I'll tell you what's up," said A.A., before Ashley had a chance to get a word in. "Ashley lied to me. She told me that Tri was desperate to stay with her and that he preferred her to me, when the opposite was true. He wanted to dump her for me, and she just couldn't bear it. It's taken her all this time to admit it! But it's too late. Our friendship is over. And as far as I'm concerned, the Ashleys are over."

"Oh my God!" Lili gasped. Lauren shook her head, looking down at the ground.

"So the question for you two is this—who are you going to choose? Me or Ashley? Because from now on, you can't be friends with us both," A.A. said.

"Excuse me?" Ashley looked aghast.

Lili looked from one to the other, as though she couldn't believe her ears. Lauren just kept staring at the ground.

But A.A. was defiant. They had to choose. If they chose to side with Ashley, so be it. She'd survive. School would be hard, but at least she'd have her dignity—and Tri.

But whatever they chose, the Ashleys were finished. Of that, A.A. was absolutely, positively certain.

"Lauren?" she demanded. "What's it going to be?"

"Well," Lauren said slowly, still looking at her feet, "Ashley is the only one of you who's apologized for not telling me about Congé. Why didn't you tell me about the change in plans?"

"Because we don't trust you!" blurted Lili, her face red. "You're not really one of us yet, however much you suck up to Ashley."

Lauren's eyes filled with tears.

"*I* trusted you," said Ashley defiantly. "I told them that you were on our side. It was Lili's idea for us to trick you. Don't even try to deny it, Lil!"

"I'm not denying anything." Lili linked her arm through A.A.'s. "I *know* who my real friends are. And I'm tired of buying shoes and bags just because you say we have to!"

"Lauren?" A.A. said again. "Me or Ashley?"

Lauren brushed her tears away with the back of her hand.

"I'm really sorry that we didn't tell you about Congé," Ashley said quickly. "A.A. and Lili talked me into it. Ask A.A. yourself if you don't believe me."

A.A. rolled her eyes.

"I didn't talk you into anything," she said. "We ALL agreed about lying to Lauren. Lili and I just explained the facts to you and—"

"So it *was* you and Lili?" Lauren interrupted. She looked shocked, as though someone had slapped her across the face. "It wasn't Ashley's idea?"

"Well—no, I guess," A.A. had to admit. One thing she wasn't, and that was a liar.

"Then I choose Ashley," said Lauren, and moved to stand next to her. The four girls—two on one side, two on another—stared at one another as if from across a great divide. The sides had been chosen. A line in the sand had been drawn. It was two against two. United they stood, divided they fell.

And that was that, thought A.A.—the end of the Ashleys.

EPILOGUES

Dear Diary,

I never thought I'd write this, but . . . I'm ~~BFF~~'s with Ashley Spencer. How weird is that? She's actually not as bad as you'd think. Sure, she's kind of bossy and a drama queen, and keeps telling me what to buy and how to wear it, and she won't shut up for a second about her love life. But the other day she totally cracked me up by making milk come out of her nose.

Still, it's a lot of pressure. When we walk into school together, everyone stops and stares. The S. Society is yesterday's news. Losing Congé and the bet really took the air out of their push-up bras. All anyone can talk about at Miss Gamble's these days is the Ashleys breakup. They can't believe it. As for me, I can't believe that Ashley and I are still friends.

Christian says I'm insane, and maybe he's right. Who'd have thought that the Ashleys would fall but that Ashley would still be standing? And that I'd be standing right next to her?

Lili and A.A. are not speaking to me at all, which is funny because they were always _much_ friendlier than Ashley to me. It's like a parallel universe.

Who knows—maybe it's a dream? When we get back from spring break I'll wake up and discover I'm still plain, frumpy, poor, and friendless.

I hope not! Stay tuned for more craziness.

Lauren Page

MEMO: FILE: DIARY: ALIOTO, ASHLEY

I'M IN BLISS. TRI IS A DOLL. LIFE AFTER
ASHLEY IS STRESS FREE. JUST 1 DARK
CLOUD. MOM SAYS WEDDING TO MARTY IS A
GO. DOES THIS MEAN MOVING TO LA-LA
LAND?
HOW DO I TELL TRI?

Hello? HELLO? Ashley here, reporting from the front lines of the war zone. I'm under attack on all sides, as usual. But I'm sure I'll come out the winner. I'm still Ashley Spencer, aren't I?

A.A. and Lili will have to give in sooner or later. They'll come crawling back. Without me, they're not the Ashleys. They're just two girls with a lot of clothes and no idea how to accessorize.

In the meantime, while I'm waiting for them to beg for forgiveness, I guess I'll hang with Lauren. She seems okay. She's practically an Ashley, and at least she didn't jump ship and race off with the S. Society when all the other rats were abandoning me. Her family is taking me with them on their trip to St. Barts over break. Her dad just bought a sweet yacht.

Speaking of ships, I can't stop thinking of Cooper in his hot uniform. I told him I'd love to be his cruise director. I'd be great at telling everyone on an ocean liner what to do. After all, I've seen *Titanic* a dozen times.

Later, skaters!

Ashley

This has been a very disturbing week. Now Max is an ex-preppie, and I'm an ex-Ashley. Hard to comprehend. It feels like I've been an Ashley all my life—literally.

I've often wondered what <u>not</u> being friends with Ashley would be like. And now I know.

Life's a little dull, I have to say. A.A. is great, but she's really preoccupied with her romance with Tri, plus she's obsessing over her mother getting married again. I'm not allowed to talk to Lauren. And Ashley is strictly off-limits.

Weird, but I kind of miss her. Who would have thought??

Yours in confusion,

Lili

ACKNOWLEDGMENTS

Thanks again to the fabulous Team Ashleys: Emily Meehan, Courtney Bongiolatti, Carolyn Pohmer, Paul Crichton, Matt Schwartz, Lucille Rettino, Valerie Shea, Brenna Sinnott, Richard Abate, Richie Kern, Melissa Myers, Paula Morris, Christina Green, and Adam Parks.

Love to everyone in my family, especially Mike & Mattie.

MWAH, MWAH, MWAH to all my readers, who are just so cute and enthusiastic!

ABOUT THE AUTHOR

When **Melissa de la Cruz** was a student at the Convent of the Sacred Heart, she never knew when Congé was going to happen, and she is still a wee bit bitter about all those nights studying for tests that were never given.

She has written many books for teens, including the bestselling series the Au Pairs, Angels on Sunset Boulevard, and Blue Bloods. She lives in Los Angeles with her husband and daughter.

Check out her website at www.melissa-delacruz.com and send her an e-mail at melissa@melissa-delacruz.com.

If you thought Ariana

was gone for good ...

you were dead wrong.

A new series from the bestselling author
of the **PRIVATE** series

Published by Simon & Schuster

love. life. heartache.

what my girlfriend doesn't know
SONYA SONES

"WINNING."—*Entertainment Weekly*

what my mothe doesn't know
SONYA SONES

★ "a satisfying, moving novel."
—*Booklist, starred*

one of those hideous books where the mother dies
SONYA SONES

From award-winning author Sonya Sones
Simon & Schuster Books for Young Readers

Get ready
for the newest
Private novel:

PARADISE LOST

Published by Simon & Schuster

And don't miss the first eight books in the Private series: